# Rise of the Dominants

RISE

 Red Phoenix

Sir's Rise: Rise of the Dominants
First Book of the Trilogy

Cover by Shanoff Designs
Formatted by BB eBooks
Phoenix symbol by Nicole Delfs

# Dedication

How exciting writing this story has been.
So I want to dedicate Sir's Rise to all of you, my fans!
We get to delve into Sir's life when he was just beginning
as a Dom, and this story only happened because of your
enthusiastic support of Brie's journey all these years.
This peek into Sir's life when he was a young man
is my gift to you.
I hope you love his story as much as I do!
You, dear friends, make writing a beautiful experience.

♥ A special dedication to MrRed's father. He passed
away while I was writing this book. He was a good man
and I loved him very much! He was so proud and
supportive of me and my work. My heart is heavy
knowing he's no longer in the world—but the love he
poured into our family lives on.
All the love for MrRed, as our family mourns the loss of
his father.

# SIGN UP FOR MY NEWSLETTER HERE FOR THE LATEST RED PHOENIX UPDATES

## SALES, GIVEAWAYS, NEW RELEASES, PREORDER LINKS, AND MORE!

### SIGN UP HERE

REDPHOENIXAUTHOR.COM/NEWSLETTER-SIGNUP

**Get the rest of the trilogy now!**

| **Master's Fate, Book 2** | **The Russian Reborn, Book 3** |
|:---:|:---:|
|  |  |

# CONTENTS

# Surprise Encounter

"*I'm sorry, son...*"

Those are the last words my father said, and they echo in my mind now as we pull up to the university. I stare out the car window, swallowing down the anger building inside me, gutted that he's not here to share in this moment.

"Wow, Thane! This is a huge campus. You sure you're not going to feel lost here?" my uncle asks, grinning as he looks at me in the reflection of the rearview mirror.

I shake my head once, frowning. I know he means well, but nothing and no one can make up for the disappointment I feel facing this day without my father—or mother.

I get out of my uncle's sedan and sling my backpack over my shoulder. I look around at other students with their parents following behind, carrying large boxes and various pieces of furniture, and shake my head in amusement.

*All the shit that's completely unnecessary for their education.*

My uncle pulls out my large suitcase while I grab the clothing bag that contains my armor against the world.

My aunt grins up at me. "Thane—"

My uncle immediately hushes her. "Remember, sweetheart, we don't call him by his first name when we're in public."

I glance around, relieved no one overheard her. I don't plan to reveal my given name to anyone here. I even toyed with legally changing my last name at one point, but I'm a Davis. I'm not about to give that up on top of everything else I've lost.

Not wanting to be recognized, I've cut off my boyishly long, dark Italian hair, replacing it with a respectable crew cut. It gives me a more businesslike appearance, and it makes me look older by several years.

With a change of location, new look, and enough time for the scandal to settle, my plan is to keep my head buried in textbooks to avoid being recognized by anyone here. The last thing I want—or need—is for my past to follow me to college. After living through two years of hell, this is my chance to break free from what happened and determine my own fucking destiny.

My aunt is positively glowing when she announces, "I baked you a fresh batch of brownies. It should help break the ice with the other boys."

I groan inwardly as she produces a massive plate from the trunk of the sedan, holding the brownies up proudly. I lay the heavy clothing bag over my suitcase, balancing it there so I can dutifully take her large plate before I turn to leave.

"Wait…don't you want us to go with you?" my uncle asks in surprise.

I turn back toward him and say in all honesty, "No, Unc."

"But…" my aunt whimpers, looking at me pleadingly before shifting her gaze to my uncle.

He looks me in the eye for several seconds, then nods his acceptance. Wrapping his arm around my aunt, he tells her in a low voice, "He needs time alone."

"But I thought we would get to see his dorm room…and meet his roommate…" she sputters.

My uncle smiles at her with compassion but shakes his head slowly.

I can tell I've hurt my aunt's feelings but, right now, I can't stomach the thought of pretending I'm okay. Especially as I watch the mothers around me hugging their adult children with tears in their eyes, while the fathers look at their sons and daughters with pride.

Those are things I will never know…

I find it far easier to simply ignore this day, getting through it the only way I know how—alone.

I start toward my assigned dorm building, only turning back when I hear my uncle's sedan driving off. As I watch the vehicle slowly disappear into the tangle of traffic, I'm hit with a sense of deep sadness. I know intellectually that I'm fortunate to have my uncle and aunt's support, but nothing can penetrate the darkness I feel inside—not even their sincere love.

Saddled with my aunt's unwieldy plate of brownies, I'm forced to wait for an opening on the crowded elevator rather than take the stairs.

I barely avoid the large plate tilting and crashing to the elevator floor when a guy squeezes into the cramped space, bumping against me just as the doors close.

While the old elevator groans in protest from the excess weight, I glance around at my fellow freshmen. It doesn't seem as if they're settling in for a simple year at college by the sheer amount of food and supplies they carry.

No, it looks like they're preparing for the apocalypse.

I smile to myself as I get off the elevator and head down the hallway. Based on all I've been through, I'm light-years ahead of my classmates and, unlike them, I'm not a person who needs pampering.

I'm here for my degree—it's the only reason I've come—and I'm hoping that my roommate shares a similar focus.

Finding my room number at the end of the hall, I open the door, still balancing my aunt's brownies. As the door slowly swings open, I'm relieved to see my room-mate hasn't arrived yet.

I lay the plate on one of the beds and survey the room. While it appears the two sides are identical, one has a better view out the small window. I immediately claim it, knowing the view from that window may save my sanity in the months to come.

To make it fair to my roommate, I switch our desks, taking the one with knife gouges that spell out the words "I love Sherry" in big letters. I chuckle to myself, unsure if the previous owner was proclaiming his love of a girl or the type of alcohol he prefers.

I push the desk up against the window and reposition the bed slightly.

Taking my suits out of the garment bag, I hang them in the small closet with care. I know a man in the business world is judged by the suit he wears, so I have been purposeful in my selection. I want my professors to know I'm not only a serious scholar, but that I intend on graduating early.

As far as I'm concerned, every day I spend in this place is a day I'm not actively advancing in my career.

I shove my suitcase under the bed and sit down at the desk that is now my home for the duration of this year. Taking out my textbooks, I look them over with interest, wanting to get a head start.

Unfortunately, on the other side of the door I hear nothing but chaos as furniture bangs against the walls and guys laugh and shout at each other while they settle in.

There's no possible way I can concentrate, so I grab the first book on the stack and slip it into my backpack. Before I leave, I write out a simple message and place the plate of brownies on the other desk, along with the note.

My aunt made these especially for you. Do with them what you like. I'll be back later. ~Davis

I'm in no mood to deal with the commotion of my roommate moving in, or the emotional goodbyes that are sure to ensue between him and his parents, and gratefully slip out of the room before they arrive.

I run down the stairs and breathe a sigh of relief the second I make it outside into the fresh air. Each step toward the library brings a greater sense of calm. Ever since the "incident" I have found my refuge—my escape—in study.

I thrive on expanding my mind because it allows me to temporarily forget what's happened. However, studying is more than just a distraction for me. The information I learn now will be used at some point in my career. This is not just an escape, but also the means by which I plan to carve out a life for myself, independent of everyone else.

I'm grateful to find the library fairly empty when I arrive. The majority of students are still either in the middle of setting up their rooms or saying goodbye to their parents, while a few are partying early to celebrate their first day on campus.

Since I have my pick of location, I settled down in the back. Taking out my Applied Calculus textbook, I begin flipping through the pages.

*Damn...*

I thrive on a good challenge and, by the looks of several of these equations, this should prove an interesting semester for me.

Fishing out a notebook from my backpack, I choose the first equation I'm unfamiliar with to see how far I can get on my own. I always use a pen whenever I do math calculations, preferring to document my thought process, rather than erase it as things become clearer.

But this math problem is even more challenging than I've anticipated. Hours into it, I look over my calculations with growing frustration, but I can't let it go.

I'm distracted when I hear two girls arguing quietly.

Looking up from my notebook, I see the library is now full of other students looking to escape, and all of us are focused on the two who are quarreling.

"I'm tired and just want to go home already…"

"Why can't you be happy for me? This is my big day, damn it," the other girl hisses. "All you ever want to do is stick your head in books."

"You know, it wouldn't hurt for you to do that once in a while."

"Don't even start, sis. Fine, be a bookworm. See if I care," she growls in disgust. "I'll just tell Mom and Dad where to find you when they're ready to leave."

"Sounds perfect to me."

"You're such a stick in the mud," she huffs, stomping off.

The library quiets down after the girl's dramatic exit, so I dive back into the equation I'm working on, but I'm soon distracted again by a soft sigh.

I look up to see the young woman has chosen to sit near me. Glancing around at the empty tables, I realize it is purposeful on her part. I look at her again to find she is blatantly staring at me.

As soon as our eyes meet, however, she looks away and adjusts her glasses with a slight smile on her lips. Her short chestnut hair frames her delicate face, emphasizing the sprinkle of freckles across her nose.

The girl has a decidedly bookish look, which I find charming. I return to my equation, quite aware of her gaze when she thinks I'm not looking.

Rather than concentrating on the math problem in front of me, I'm now focusing on her. Another glance in her direction and this time I hold her gaze. She doesn't look away as the sexual tension builds between us.

I make no move toward her, smirking as I look down at my equation again. She's proven a worthy distraction, and I can no longer concentrate.

The girl lets out a long sigh, chewing absently on her pencil as she pretends to read the book in front of her—but, I suspect she has other things on her mind.

I watch with interest as she gives me a flirtatious grin, adjusting her glasses before getting up and heading to the reference section of the library. She's wearing a midline skirt that is conservative but still sways enticingly as she walks away.

A few minutes later, taking her cue, I set down my pen and leave my calculations on the table. Surveying the other students, I note they all seem preoccupied and not are watching what I'm doing.

The librarian, however, stares at me intently as I walk past her. I give her a slight nod, acknowledging her station, and watch with satisfaction as she blushes.

Heading deep into the reference section, I find my chestnut beauty hidden in the back. A smile spreads across her face as I approach, but when she opens her mouth to speak, I put my finger on those pink lips and shake my head.

There will be no words between us.

I replace my finger with my lips, pressing my mouth against hers. Kissing her gently at first, I feel her body respond to mine, and I slip my tongue into her mouth.

She moans softly so I pull away, shaking my head. The only way this continues is if she stays totally silent.

Looking at me with those sultry eyes, she tilts her chin up, begging for another kiss.

I claim her sensual lips again while my hand begins exploring her curves. As my hand moves downward, I grasp her waist, pulling her against me so she can feel my growing excitement.

It has been a while since I've felt the thrill of penetration, and my cock aches in anticipation of it.

Hiking up her skirt, I push her back against the shelves, the scent of old books surrounding us as I feel between her legs. Her panties are already wet, letting me know she'd been fantasizing about this encounter ever since she sat down next to me.

*Naughty girl…*

I slip my hand under the thin material and struggle not to groan when I feel the slick warmth of her pussy. My cock grows even harder.

Knowing time is of the essence, I slip her panties down and unzip my jeans. I pull a condom from my wallet and watch her eyes widen as I roll it down over my hard shaft.

Sliding the head of my cock against her tight opening, I take a few moments to build up her sexual desire. The sound of a low cough echoing from somewhere in the library only adds to the excitement of what we are about to do.

Looking deep into her eyes, I lift her leg to open her pussy to me and slowly push my cock into her hot depths.

She makes the barest of sounds and I immediately pull out, raising an eyebrow. Looking at me desperately, she bites her lip to show she's serious about keeping silent, her eyes begging me to continue.

I kiss those pink lips again as I slide my shaft back into her, pushing even deeper. She trembles with need when I begin thrusting. The excitement of having sex in the college library has both our hearts racing.

The small beads of perspiration on her skin cause those sexy glasses to slip down the bridge of her nose. I take them off and carefully set them on a shelf before gripping onto her buttocks tight. I begin stroking her deeper while keeping eye contact as I climb toward climax.

I want her to climax too, so I pull out slightly, reach down between her legs and play with her swollen clit while I continue to thrust into her with my hard cock.

Unfortunately, the cougher seems to be on the move and, by the sound of it, he's headed straight toward us.

It seems the idea of being caught turns my chestnut beauty on, because her pupils grow wider just before I feel her pussy squeeze my shaft with her orgasm. My body instinctually responds, thrusting deeper as I follow with my own climax.

I quickly pull out, slipping my cock back into my pants, condom and all. She barely has time to pull up her panties and fix her skirt before our coughing intruder walks by our section.

I lean into her, kissing her passionately to hide the reason for her panting breath, then turn to give the guy a hard stare, letting him know he's interrupted us.

He shrugs, giving me an apologetic grin before covering his mouth and wandering off amid another bout of coughing.

I look down at her and smile as I gently place the glasses back on her face. Giving her one last kiss, I signal that she should leave first. She glances back at me with that coy grin just before disappearing around the corner.

I head to the restroom before returning to the table, and am surprised to see she is gone. As a parting gift, however, she has left her pencil—nibble marks and all—resting on my Calculus book.

I immediately slip it into my pocket, keeping the memento to remember my first campus tryst.

Hell, if this is what college has to offer, getting through the next few years won't be so tedious after all...

# Roommates

I return to my dorm in a much happier state. I notice the door to the room is open, but when I peek inside, I don't see anyone. Slowly closing the door behind me, I walk toward my bed. I nearly jump out of my skin when I hear a freakishly loud crack beside my ear.

I immediately turn to see a young man holding a leather whip. He bursts out laughing.

"Oh, hell, if you could have seen the look on your face just now…"

"*What the fuck!*" I complain.

With a smirk on his face, he curls up his whip and places it on the desk. "My name is Brad. I'm your roommate for the year."

Although he holds out his hand to me, I don't make a move to shake it.

"Ah, come on…don't be like that. I was just having a little fun." He glances at the whip. "Myrtle didn't mean any harm. She's just a little thing with a loud bark."

"What kind of person brings a whip to college?" I

demand.

He holds out his hand again. "I'll tell ya just as soon as you take my hand and introduce yourself."

I study him for a second, noting the gleam of amusement in his eye. I can tell by the honest look in his gaze that he's not a dick, despite what just happened, so I shake his hand. "You can call me Davis."

He shakes it back vigorously. "Shouldn't you and I be on a first name basis since we're going to be living together for the year?"

"No. I prefer to be called by my last name."

He chuckles as he lets go of my hand. "Fine, you can call me Anderson, if you want, but I'm going to call you buddy since we're roomies. Just seems natural where I'm from."

"And where are you from?"

He breaks out in a huge smile as he picks up the whip again. "Myrtle and me are from Greeley, Colorado. Land of blue skies with the great Rocky Mountains as our playground."

"Can't say I've ever heard of it, but I know of Denver. Flown through there once on my way to California."

"Yep, we're a little over an hour north of there."

Staring at his miniature bullwhip, I ask, "I take it Greeley is a rural town?"

"You'd be mistaken to think that. It's a modern city, but we definitely take pride in our country roots, and my family still owns a ranch on the outskirts of it."

I nod, staring at his leather whip. "Is that why you brought that?"

He smirks. "No. I brought Myrtle to impress the

girls."

I raise my eyebrow. "With that small thing?"

Before I can even react, he flicks the whip again, cracking it next to my ear. Even though I stand my ground, my heart races at the sound of it.

Anderson snorts. "Size doesn't matter when you know how to use the equipment."

My eyes naturally go to his crotch, thinking he must be compensating. But then I note the sizeable bulge in his pants—quite the opposite of what I was expecting.

He sets down his whip and points to the empty plate of brownies. "Just wanted to say thanks for those."

My jaw drops. "You ate all of them?"

"Oh, heck no. My sisters devoured them in no time flat."

"How many sisters do you have?"

"Would you believe me if I said eight?"

"Wow…" I can't imagine what that must be like, having been raised an only child.

"Well, I don't. I was only joking. I have three, which is more than enough, I can assure you—but I adore each one, don't get me wrong." He looks down at the empty plate sadly. "Despite the fact they demolished the brownie plate your aunt so thoughtfully made for me."

"Three girls ate all of those?" I ask in disbelief, knowing how many there were.

"To be honest, I had a few, as did Mom and Pop."

"Your whole family came from Colorado to see you off?"

"Oh, heck, yeah. One for all, and all for one in my family."

I nod, even more grateful I wasn't here when they all came barging in.

"So, where have you been? My sisters stayed extra-long hoping to meet you."

"Sorry. I've been at the library studying."

"Why?" he laughed. "We have the whole school year to stick our noses in books."

I cock my head, telling him in all seriousness, "Study is the only reason we're here."

He shakes his head, chuckling. "No, it is *not* the only reason."

"Why are you here, then?"

"I want to experience everything college has to offer, including the incredible selection of girls on this campus."

"So, you are telling me that you only came for the women?"

"Not just the women. I plan to do some major partying, as well."

I shift my feet, disappointed to discover my roommate and I are complete opposites.

He looks me over and grins, motioning to my collar. "I see you weren't just studying at that library."

I pull at my collar and notice a smudge of pink lipstick. I can't help but smile, thinking back on my encounter.

"You and I are more alike than you think," Anderson insists.

"I won't deny I enjoy the company of a woman, but I'm here for one sole purpose—to get my degree as quickly and efficiently as possible. Life is out there," I say, pointing toward the window. "This…here…is just a means to an end."

Anderson shakes his head. "You got it all wrong, buddy."

"We'll see," I answer, knowing I'm not going to win the argument with him at this point.

He holds out his hand to me. "Let's make a bet. At the end of this year, we'll revisit this conversation and see if you've had a change of heart."

I snort. "What's in it for me?"

He shrugs. "What do you want?"

"If I haven't changed my focus, you agree to take a class of my choosing during your sophomore year."

He pulls his hand back. "Oh, hell, no!"

I smirk. "Then you're admitting I'm right."

He holds his hand back out, grinning. "I'll take your bet, Davis. If you lose, you agree to party with me for an entire weekend. No books allowed."

I take his hand and shake firmly. "Hope you like Applied Calculus."

Anderson throws his head back and laughs.

Even though we are polar opposites, I like this guy. I can tell by the intensity of his gaze that Anderson is sharp. He just hasn't realized his potential yet.

"So, Davis, you against drinking altogether?"

"No."

"Good to hear," he says with a mischievous grin as he reaches under his bed and pulls out a storage trunk. Opening it, he digs under the clothes and produces a fine bottle of aged whiskey. I raise my eyebrow as he places it on his desk and reaches back in, producing two glasses.

"My granddad sent this along with me with strict instructions it only be used for solemn occasions."

My own father used to share his love of wine with me. Being of Italian descent, he thought nothing of serving me a glass at formal meals, even when I was quite young. He always claimed a good wine enhanced a meal, and he didn't want me to miss out on the flavors it produced. So, as far as I'm concerned, drinking alcohol is purely a palate enhancer.

I watch as Anderson breaks the seal on the bottle and pours out two shots. Handing me a glass, he smiles as he holds up his. "This is to formally seal our bet."

I knock my glass against his and swallow the unique, smoky flavor. It burns slightly, but this is a smooth, high-end whiskey that goes down easily.

"Ahh…" Anderson sighs in satisfaction after taking a drink. "Damn, my granddad spoiled me with this one."

I take another drink myself, nodding my head. "Exceptional."

He glances at me and that charismatic smile returns. "I think you and I are going to have fun this year."

I chuckle into my glass as I take the last sip and place it on the desk. "I hope you enjoy advanced math, Anderson. That's what I see in your future."

"Bwahaha…" he bellows as he lies down on his bed.

Anderson looks over at his mini-fridge, then his gaze moves to his TV and microwave oven before glancing at my sparse living space. "What's up with the lack of furnishings? Your parents coming with the rest tomorrow?"

I have to keep my emotions in check, answering him

in a casual tone, "I believe in simple living."

"Oh, like a monk or something?"

I smile slightly. "Something like that."

"You're a strange one, Davis. Makes me want to meet those parents of yours."

I cannot hide my frown. "My parents aren't something I talk about—ever."

"Gotcha." He folds his arms behind his head as he stares at my empty space. "How about siblings? Got any of those?"

I give him a sideways glance.

"Wow, you and I couldn't come from more different backgrounds. You're damn lucky I'm here."

"How so?" I answer drolly.

"You've been living a sad little existence without me."

I snort. "You don't know anything about me, Anderson."

He sits up and looks me in the eye. "Go ahead, then. Tell me everything."

I shake my head, deciding to pull out my notebook to look at that damned equation again. It's better I keep my distance and stick to my original plan.

Putting my earphones on, I ignore him as I delve back in, determined to conquer the math equation on my own terms.

I feel a tap on my shoulder and turn to look up at him as I lift my earphones. "What?"

He grins down at me. "I'm not the enemy, buddy."

"I never said you were."

"Look, you can trust me. Whatever you're trying to

hide from…I want you to know you're safe with me. I'm loyal to a fault—at least, that's what my mama claims."

"I'll keep that in mind," I say as I slip my headphones back on.

It would be nice to have someone I could trust, but I can't take that chance.

I glance over at the miniature bullwhip still sitting on his desk and smile to myself. While we may be polar opposites, I appreciate having an interesting roommate.

# The Russian

My schedule begins with three classes every Monday. The first two focus on my interest in math, Applied Calculus and Financial Accounting, but the last is a science course. Although it has no practical application as far as my business degree is concerned, science is required for all underclassmen and I find biology fascinating.

Having tested out of the more rudimentary classes in high school, I've chosen Molecular Biology. Understanding life on a microscopic level should prove enlightening.

When I enter the science classroom, I settle down in the second row of tables. It's close enough to see and hear the professor clearly, but without being under her direct scrutiny.

As the class begins to fill up, I receive a few sideways glances. It's obvious by my youthful appearance that I'm an underclassman, and this is a class designed for the upperclassmen.

I take pride in my ability to advance through my

courses quickly. It's one reason I've looked forward to college. It wasn't easy enduring the judgments of my peers in high school because of my intellect and drive.

In this new environment, both will be rewarded.

A calmness settles over the room as the professor walks up to the front and the students prepare for our class to begin.

That's when *he* enters the room like a whirlwind of energy.

All eyes turn toward the door as he swings it open. The quiet of the room is broken by a boisterous spurt of foreign phrases as a muscular kid with a shaven head finishes flirting with a group of girls walking in the hallway.

Their excited giggles echo down the hall as he shuts the door.

Our professor, however, is less than amused and stares him down silently.

He gives her a respectable nod, then surveys the room with his piercing blue eyes. I note how the girls smile and turn their heads shyly. But, when our eyes meet, I hold his gaze.

My heart rate increases for some unexplainable reason. He grins at me before heading to the back of the class.

Our professor stares at him for several seconds before turning around and writing on the whiteboard.

I turn in my seat slightly so I can give the guy another once over, curious about which country he's from. Having traveled the world with my father as a boy, I'm familiar with a variety of languages, but I have only mastered a few.

Although I'm not familiar with the words he spoke, it sounds Slavic in origin to me. Based on his facial features which are defined by a thinner, pronounced nose, a defined chin, and contoured lips, I narrow it down to Ukrainian or Russian.

He appears to ignore us all as he stares out the window, looking bored as Dr. Barr goes over the class syllabus, emphasizing the extensive lab work required.

I have zero issues with the additional lab work. I'm looking forward to the thrill of discovery as I run tests on various microorganisms over the semester. With a quick glance around the room, I start assessing the other students to ensure I get an appropriate lab partner.

Before the class ends, Dr. Barr tells us to pick our partner for the duration of the course. I start walking toward a scholarly looking upperclassman up in the front. Unfortunately, before I can take another step, the person sitting next to him chooses the guy. I gaze around the room and notice that people are quickly pairing up without giving me a second glance. It has to be my age, and I growl under my breath.

I feel a slap on the back, follow by an amused chuckle.

I turn around, watching his blue eyes glint with self-assuredness as he grabs my hand and shakes it vigorously. I have not agreed to be partners with this man, but a quick scan of the room verifies everyone else has chosen their lab partners.

"Comrade," he states enthusiastically. The briny odor of pickles hovers around him, and I suspect he's been drinking.

"Are you Russian?"

He points to his chest and says with a proud grin, "*Da*, Russian!"

"Do you speak English?"

He looks at me questioningly.

I know a few words in Russian, but my vocabulary is limited to only the basics needed for getting around in a foreign country. So I ask him the standard 'Do you speak English'.

"*Ty govorish' po-angliyski?*"

He smiles proudly as he shakes his head no.

*Great...*

The small amount of Russian I know won't work in an educational environment. I'm seriously fucked by having this guy as a lab partner and, based on by the shit-eating grin on his face, he agrees.

The other students start filing out of the classroom, letting Dr. Barr know whom they have partnered with as they leave. Once the class has cleared out, she looks over at me. "Mr. Davis, am I correct in assuming you've chosen Mr. Durov as your partner?"

"I think *choose* is an overstatement."

She turns her attention on Durov. "Are you satisfied with Mr. Davis as your lab partner this semester?"

He just answers her with a bemused smirk.

Dr. Barr turns back to me, stating matter-of-factly, "Fortunately, the language of science is not limited by dialect." Her statement lets me know I have no choice in the matter.

*Lucky me...*

I follow Durov out of class and watch the reactions of the girls as he passes. It's almost as if his aura is a physical presence they cannot ignore. Time and time again, as he walks by, the girls look up almost as if they can sense him.

I have never seen anything like it. Even though he may be useless as my biology partner, I look forward to studying him outside of class.

He disappears among the throng of students while I head off to my dorm room to decompress after my first day.

To my chagrin, as I get out my key to the room, I find a piece of tape covering the lock. Leaning closer, I can hear the faint giggles of a young woman just before she gasps, "Oh, Brad…"

I pull away, not wanting to hear any more. Anderson and I haven't even had time to talk about having girls over, and he's already sampling the freshmen inventory.

I shake my head as I leave. Hell, at this rate, he'll be through a fair amount of them by Christmas.

I change direction and head to the library. The Los Angeles sky seems particularly blue and free of smog today. Appreciating the rarity of it, I stand outside in the sun for several minutes before heading into the building. As I enter, I notice a girl with long, blonde hair staring at me intently. The look is not flirtatious, but one of extreme interest.

I don't know her and it sets me on edge. Not wanting the girl to get any closer and possibly recognize who I am, I hurry inside to avoid further contact, finding refuge in a secluded section of the library.

To my relief, she doesn't follow, leaving me to concentrate on my work.

Considering this is only my first day, I'm surprised by the amount of homework I've already been assigned. It appears my decision to start college a year earlier was an excellent one. There's no chance of getting bored here, the way I was in high school.

I plan to start with accounting first. I like that my two business classes complement each other, and I can see that playing out well this semester.

Biology, however…

I hope I don't end up regretting the class. The last thing I want is to carry someone through an entire semester—I did that enough in high school.

Still, I'm intrigued by the Russian.

However, if we are to have any hope of completing our labs, I'll have to communicate effectively. With that in mind, I get up and search the language section. Finding a book on the rudiments of the Russian dialect, and one specifically written to teach English speakers Russian, I head to the checkout desk.

"I see you are taking Russian. Pretty ambitious," the librarian comments. "Let me suggest one more book." Her fingers dance on the keyboard as she looks up the book's location and instructs me to wait. A few minutes later, she returns with an old book with a loose spine.

"I know it looks a little worse for wear, but it's the best."

I smile in gratitude. "Thank you."

I see that blush return to her cheeks, the same color as on my first visit here. While it's somewhat disconcerting having a woman old enough to be my mother reacting so strongly to me, I can't deny an attraction to her.

*What guy hasn't fantasized about a librarian?*

I don't want to complicate things between us, however, as I take the book from her, I look into those dark brown eyes and make a silent promise. If she's still interested when I'm ready to graduate, we will indulge in our mutual attraction for each other.

Returning to my seat, I open the old book and begin skimming the pages. This is exactly what I need. A problem solver at heart, I'm not about to let our language barrier be the difference between me getting an A or failing.

Pushing my homework aside for the moment, I dive into the book. That Russian kid won't know what hit him.

# Solidarity

I don't head back to the dorm until way past dinner and, by then, I've forgotten to eat. My stomach growls the moment I enter the room and smell fresh popcorn. I watch as Anderson empties the last of the contents of the microwave bag into his mouth.

When my stomach growls again, he looks up. "Sorry, buddy. I would have saved you some if I'd known you were hungry." He shows me the empty bag. "This was my last one."

"Not your problem," I assure him, feeling foolish for not making it to the cafeteria before it closed. I sit down on my bed, ignoring the grumble of my stomach.

Anderson gets up and starts rummaging through his closet. "I may not have popcorn, but I've got something even better. Never fear."

"Don't bother. It's my own fault."

He looks back at me. "You never skip a meal if you want to stay on top of your game."

I give him a half-hearted smile as an especially painful growl cuts through my mid-region. "Sometimes, I get lost in my studies and forget everything around me."

"You know, I can't say that has ever happened to me—not even once," he chuckles as he gets out a bowl and fills it with water. He throws in a dried noodle mix from a package before shoving it in the microwave and hitting Start.

"Well, it's happened to me more times than I want to admit, but I normally have access to food when I realize it."

He nods toward my empty area. "Yeah, you didn't really come prepared for college life, did you? But that's okay. I've got your back."

Anderson pulls the bowl out of the microwave and stirs it before handing the steaming concoction over to me. "Nothing like a hot bowl of ramen."

I look down at it and snort. "I've heard this is the official food of college students."

"Hey, this isn't that cheap stuff. I only go to authentic Asian shops to get it. That other stuff..." He shudders. "It shouldn't even be called ramen."

I laugh. "What? Do you only eat gourmet or something?"

"I take cooking seriously, buddy. Nothing wrong with that."

I smile as I watch another layer of his personality peel away. "Never said there was. My own father cooked a mean Ribollita."

"An excellent Italian dish."

I'm surprised Anderson knows the Tuscan dish. Not wanting him to delve into my own family history, I ask,

"Who taught you about food?"

"My mama taught me everything I know about cooking, and she told me that LA has an incredible range of cuisine to sample. It's part of the reason I chose this school...in addition to all the California girls, of course," he adds with a cheeky grin.

The ramen is still too hot to eat. But I'm starving, so I blow on it, struggling to remain patient. "Does that mean you came here to learn cooking management?"

Anderson laughs. "Hell no. Cooking is just a pastime of mine. No way would you find me slaving away in a restaurant kitchen."

I finally take my first sip of the soup, expecting to be hit with copious amounts of salt, but the spicy miso broth is actually quite pleasant, and the rehydrated bits of vegetables and mushrooms have retained their natural texture. I look up at him in surprise. "This is actually good."

"The Japanese know ramen."

Another angry growl erupts from my stomach in protest to my leisurely eating.

"Go ahead. Shove it in. No need to hold back," Anderson assures me.

I decide to take him at his word and slurp up the noodles the way I've seen the Japanese do on my father's Asian tour. I was told it was considered good manners in that country.

"That was seriously good," I tell him after sipping the last drop of broth from the bowl.

"I can make you another. It's the least I can do after kicking you out of our room without warning."

I hold a hand up. "No, I'm good." Glancing at his side of the room, I see no telltale signs of his afternoon tryst. "I made it a point to stay away as long as I could."

Anderson snorts with amusement. "You could have saved yourself the trouble. She wasn't here that long."

"What? Things didn't go well? She sounded perfectly happy when I dropped by."

He arches an eyebrow. "Everything was proceeding as planned. I had her all nice and juicy after a satisfying tongue session, but the minute I pulled my cock out, she completely froze."

"Really? I assume by the way girls talk that they all lust after big dicks."

"They may lust after them, but I never know how they'll react until they actually see what I have to offer face to face."

I can just imagine a girl staring wide-eyed, like a deer in the headlights, as he pulls out his large shaft for the first time.

"Needless to say, they tend to eat those words," he adds with a chuckle.

I shake my head. "Never would have guessed."

"Thankfully, most girls are more than happy to suck me off, but getting a deep fucking? That is always the hope, but it's an extreme rarity for me." Anderson looks down at his crotch, shaking his head sadly.

I laugh in response, but I can appreciate his plight. Not to enjoy the unspeakable pleasure of a warm, wet pussy wrapped around your shaft when you come— that's a tragedy in any man's book.

No wonder he's seeking to couple with as many girls

as he can.

"So basically, you're on the hunt to find the right Cinderella to fit your massive *shoe*."

Anderson surprises me when he starts howling in laughter. He's so loud, the guys on the other side of the wall start knocking against it, demanding that he shut up.

He wipes away tears as he swallows down his mirth, shaking a finger at me. "Gotta admit, I never thought of it like that before."

"Now that I understand the full girth of the situation, I'm sure we can work out a system so you can try on as many slippers as you need."

Chuckling, he tells me, "Works both ways, buddy. Feel free to bring your lady friends up here. I'll promise you two things: I won't go after your women, and I won't listen at the door, no matter how tempted I am."

I snort humorously. "I can assure you, I won't be bringing anyone up. I have no interest in personal relationships."

"Don't tell me you're one of those scholarly types who doesn't believe in love? Hell, don't you know that love makes the world go round?" Anderson states with a teasing grin.

"I'm not saying it doesn't exist. It just isn't for me."

"That whole monk thing again?"

"It's more like...self-protection."

"Been hurt bad by a girl, huh?"

"Not even close."

If I'd been thinking, I would have said yes, then Anderson would have dropped it. Instead, he proceeds to take out his aged whiskey and pours us both a drink. "So, what happened?"

"You shouldn't waste that stuff," I tell him.

"It's not wasting when I really want to know." He hands me a glass. He tips his drink to me and lets out a satisfied sigh, savoring the first sip.

I stare at the amber liquid for a moment before swallowing. Anderson's easy charm seems to have a way of pulling me in against my will.

After taking a drink, I stare at him. I trust my instincts and feel no hidden agenda behind his interest. The fact is, I'll need someone to have my back when shit hits the fan. Thinking back on that blonde today, I decide it's better to be on the offensive.

Enjoying the warmth of the smoky malt, I tell him, "I have no parents."

"Gah…" Anderson gasps, his green eyes flashing with a mix of sympathy and pain. "You're an orphan?"

"By choice. My uncle offered to adopt me, but I would have ruined their lives. God, I was so angry back then…"

"That's not right," he mutters.

"What? That I have no parents, or that I chose solitude over family?"

He looks me in the eye. "Both, if I'm being honest." Anderson shakes his head in disbelief, muttering, "I have an abundance of family. Parents, sisters, grandparents, cousins, second cousins, aunts and uncles…you name it. I can't imagine my life without their support."

"You only think that because it's what you know," I reply. Taking another draught of the whiskey, I think back to the huge family gatherings we used to have on

*Isola d' Elba*. I had experienced the stability and strength of *familia* once—only to have it ripped away.

Like Anderson, there was a time I thought I couldn't live without them, but the fact that I'm here now is proof otherwise. Amazing what the human spirit can endure when forced.

"Do you believe you make your own destiny?" I ask him. I'm leading him with the question, knowing there's only one right answer.

He seems a little thrown by it, but answers, "Ah, yeah…sure…" Then he adds, "However, it doesn't hurt to have a posse behind you."

I like his answer and hold up my glass to him before finishing the last of the whiskey and setting it on the desk.

Without missing a beat, he pours me more.

"Stop wasting it," I complain. "Your grandfather meant it for you, not me."

His grin widens as he pours another splash into my tumbler and pushes it toward me. "You can't tell me what to do, Davis."

I shake my head, chuckling as I pick it up. "I trust you on a gut level, Anderson, and I can count the number of people I trust on one hand."

"I'm honored," he replies, holding up his glass to me.

"Know that I have your back, as well."

He grins. "Appreciate it, Davis."

"And I'll do everything in my power to support your endeavor in finding your perfect *fit*…"

Anderson smirks. "And I promise to keep that damn

secret of yours—whatever it is."

My smiles falters as bright red blood flashes before my eyes and that horrifying scene begins to play out in my head. I suddenly realize I'm not ready to tell him anything. Hell, I've spent years in counseling, and I still can't face the memories of that day—much less voice them aloud to him.

Pushing back the bloody vision, I confess, "I need more time."

Anderson stares hard at me, eventually nodding. "When you're ready, Davis, I'll carry that burden with you."

# Laundry

I only have one extra class on Friday, Photography 101. Although it has no direct application to business, I need it to meet my arts and humanities requirement and can see the advantage of understanding composition in regards to marketing.

I enter the classroom and immediately realize I'm in the wrong place. The room is filled with the smell of incense, and a soothing chime sounds in the background. I head back out and recheck my schedule. Looking at the room number again, I'm dismayed to see they match, but I assume the photography class has moved.

Returning inside, I scan the room, looking for the professor. I finally settle on the woman dressed in a bright purple muumuu who is swaying to the music.

"Are you the professor here?" I ask her as I approach.

She looks up at me with a relaxed smile. "Yes...I am."

"Where has the photography class been moved to?"

"It didn't move."

I silently groan, realizing this *is* the class I signed up for. "Then I take it you are Professor Brooks?" I state, holding out my hand to her.

She takes my hand, her smile growing wider.

I glance around the room uncomfortably, feeling completely out of my element in this liberal arts class. The others must sense it, too, because I can feel their disdain as they stare at my white shirt and tie.

Professor Brooks takes my arm. "Why don't you sit up front? The vibe feels right for you."

I sit down reluctantly, already contemplating heading straight to the registrar office to drop the class.

I'm startled to see the blonde who was staring at me the other day stride into the classroom. As soon as she enters, she stops short and scowls at the burning incense. She quickly turns to make a quick exit, but Professor Brooks is too fast for her.

Taking her by the arm, she steers her in my direction. The blonde is dressed as conservatively as I am, and looks equally out of place.

"Seems to me, you two have a lot in common," the professor states as she seats the blonde beside me.

I stare intently at the girl, waiting to see if there's a spark of recognition when our eyes meet, but I see only a look of utter shock on her face.

She quickly recovers, settling into her seat and getting out her notebook. I can tell, however, that she is acutely aware of my presence by the way she keeps licking her lips and moving nervously in her chair.

Although she is stunning with that long blonde hair

and those perfectly arched lips, I don't feel any attraction toward her—which I find odd.

Even with my curiosity piqued, I still plan to drop the class and avoid having further contact with the girl.

My decision made, I turn my attention back to Professor Brooks and am surprised to find myself drawn into her lecture. While her teaching methods may be unorthodox, there is no disputing her years of professional experience as a field photographer or the deep passion she has for sharing that extensive experience with our class of novices.

By the time the hour is through, Professor Brooks has won me over. Despite having zero personal interest in photography before this class, she has me looking forward to attending next Friday. "Your only assignment for the week is to take a single subject photo that speaks to you personally. I don't care what the subject is as long as it is something you feel passionate about in some way. Heck, it can even be your lunch." Laughter follows. "What I want is to see a glimpse of the world through your eyes. That's the magic of a photo."

The blonde pops out of her seat as soon as Professor Brooks dismisses the class and heads straight toward the door.

I stay behind, wanting to thank Professor Brooks. Shaking her hand, I tell her, "I look forward to the semester ahead."

Rather than shaking my hand this time, she pats it gently. "I'm glad to hear it. I have a suspicion you have an eye for structure. It will be interesting to see how it plays out in your photos."

"Really?"

She nods. "I have this sense about people."

I can't explain what it is about Professor Brooks, but I feel both challenged and relaxed around her.

As I start to leave, she says, "I recommend you wear something a little looser next class. You're going to need to move freely."

I cock my head. "Meaning?"

She just gives me an amused smile.

Truly, Professor Brooks is unlike any teacher I've ever had. I leave the classroom feeling revitalized, despite the lingering odor of incense that follows me.

Before I'm out of the building, I'm accosted by the blonde in the hallway.

Grabbing my arm, she demands, "Can I talk to you for a moment?"

Not interesting in causing a scene, I walk her over to a secluded area. "Why are you stalking me?"

When she frowns, those shapely lips turn down flirtatiously, even though her eyes do not reflect those feelings. I wonder if she's even aware of it.

"I haven't been stalking you," she insists.

"Then explain why you were staring me down outside the library, and suddenly show up in my class today?"

"Okay, I'll admit to staring at you, but you would, too if you were me."

"Explain."

She looks extremely uncomfortable when she answers. "You remind me of someone."

I don't like playing these games and demand,

"Who?"

I fully expect her to say my given name, so I'm unprepared when I hear, "You bear a strong resemblance to my brother. It's eerie how much you look like him."

"Okay…"

She lowers her eyes for a moment before meeting my gaze. "He died a few years ago."

The pain in her eyes rekindles my own, and I am suddenly overcome with sympathy for the girl. "I can only imagine the pain you must feel."

Tears start welling in her eyes, but she shakes her head slightly and wills them away, explaining, "Joseph wouldn't want me to cry."

"I'm sure he would understand."

She wipes any remaining wetness and meets my gaze again. "It's strange how alike you are. Even your voice reminds me of him."

"I'm sorry for your loss," I reply, shifting my feet, put off by the ghostly role she's forced me into.

The girl seems to realize how unnerved I feel and smiles apologetically. "I really didn't mean to stare, but I can't help myself. I miss Joseph…"

The depth of loss I see in her eyes draws out my protective side. I feel a connection to her because of our shared pain. Holding out my hand, I formally introduce myself. "I'm Davis. And you are?"

She stares at my hand for a moment before taking it. I can feel her whole body trembling as she squeezes my hand to shake it. "I'm Samantha."

"Last name?"

"Clark."

"Would you like to get some coffee, Clark?"

She hesitates for only a second before answering, "Yes. I would like that."

As we walk toward the campus café, I note the way she hunches her shoulders, clutching her books as if in defense against the world—it only serves to make me feel more protective of her.

I try to buy her a cup, but she insists on buying it for herself. "I won't be beholden to any man."

I chuckle to myself. While I appreciate her conviction, I'm grateful I have no designs on her. I suspect Clark could prove a real heartbreaker.

As we sit drinking our coffee, I catch her staring at me several times. At one point, she even reaches out to touch my jaw, stating in wonder, "It's like he's here."

I take her hand and set it gently on the table. "I am not him, and as cruel as this may sound, I am not willing to play your brother's ghost."

She snatches her hand away, muttering, "Of course not. I should leave…"

I stop her when she tries to get up and guide her back down to the chair. "If we are going to have a class together, we need to address this now so it doesn't become more awkward between us."

She nods. "Wise."

I give her an amused look. "Isn't that a term used for old men?"

Clark laughs lightly. "What would you prefer…judicious?"

I sit back and nod my approval.

"How do we make this work? What exactly do you

want me to do?" she asks with a slight rise in her voice, belying her apprehension.

"It's simple," I assure her. "Get to know me the same as you would any other person. Do *not* put your brother's attributes on me. If something I do reminds you of him, don't tell me—keep it to yourself. Continually remind yourself I am not him. Don't let your mind fool yourself into thinking any different."

She takes in a deep breath and lets it out slowly, still looking pensive.

"It's not hard, but it will take constant vigilance on your part."

Clark narrows her eyes as she stares at me intently, her gaze darting around my face as she takes in every detail. No one has ever scrutinized me like this before, but I take it in stride, knowing she needs to note the differences between us. I hear her whispering to herself, "You are not Joseph…"

I nod my agreement.

I see tears start to form in her eyes again, but she closes them. When she opens them again, the tears are gone. Clark stares at me as she takes a casual sip of coffee.

"We're good?" I ask her.

"Yes." Clark glances at her watch and suddenly stands up, grabbing her purse and books. "Hate to run, Davis, but I've got one more class today."

"No rest for the wicked, huh?" I tease.

She turns, her lips curling into a charming smirk. "Never."

As I watch her leave, I note that she isn't hunched

over her books as severely as before. I hope our little chat has helped because I suspect, based on our short time together, that she could make a good ally.

When I return to the dorm room, I'm still plagued by the smell of incense. Ripping off my clothes, I grab my duffle bag and stuff them in. As much as I like the professor, I could seriously do without this stench following me home.

Slipping on my black sweat pants, I head down to the laundry room in the basement. I'm not surprised to find the laundry room is empty on a Friday afternoon. I start up the washer and open the door to head upstairs, but I unexpectedly crash into a young Asian woman carrying a large basket.

"Whoa…" I exclaim, catching her basket before it falls to the floor. I can't hide the look of surprise on my face. Females are not allowed to use the laundry room in our building.

Her cheeks redden as she blurts out a quick explanation. "No one is normally here on Fridays…" I tilt my head, giving her a stern look and enjoy watching the deepening of her blush as she stammers, "The girls' laundry is always packed…I have to wait for hours."

As she continues her explanation, I look her over. I suspect she's a few years older than me but she's tiny in stature, her head barely coming up to my chest. The golden tone of her skin contrasts charmingly with her straight black hair and alluring dark eyes.

"So, I decided to take matters into my own hands, and for the last year I've been doing my laundry over here. I don't see the harm when no one's here."

I raise an eyebrow.

"Except you…of course."

I can't help but smile when I see how disappointed she looks when she turns to leave.

"I have no problem with it," I tell her.

The girl looks back at me with a hopeful look. "Really?"

I shrug. "Why would I care when there are plenty of unused washers here."

The smile returns to her face as she walks over to one of the washers, and fills it with half her basket, then stuffs the rest in the next one. After she has both running, she faces me.

"I always stay to watch over my clothes because I can't chance someone finding my stuff and kicking me out permanently. I'd be happy to watch over yours as well, handsome stranger."

I noticed her eyes aren't leaving my naked chest and smirk. "That would be totally unnecessary but, if you would like some company, I'm not opposed to staying."

Her eyes slowly travel from my chest up to my face. "Actually…I've always fantasized about having sex in this laundry room after spending hours upon hours alone here. Have you?"

"I haven't—until now."

The sexual tension in the room instantly rises as she moves closer. Tentatively placing her hands on my chest, she stands on tiptoes and purses her lips.

I gladly accept her invitation and lean down to kiss her, feeling gratified when I hear her murmur, "Oh, God, those lips…"

Needing no further encouragement, I lift her up and set her on the washer. Trailing my tongue lightly over her bottom lip, I hesitate for a moment before kissing her again.

She leans forward, parting her lips slightly in anticipation.

I kiss her deeply, evoking a passionate moan from her. The sound of her excitement, coupled with the softness of those lips, has my cock aching with desire.

But I want her wet and ready for me, so I slip my hands under her shirt and play with her nipples. She leans into my caress and begs softly, "Pinch them."

Based on my prior experience with females, I only squeeze them lightly as I continue to kiss her.

"Harder," she begs.

For some unknown reason, her request turns me on and I groan as I roll her hard nipples between my fingers with greater force.

She gasps in pleasure, crying, "Oh, fuck yeah…!"

Needing to feel her pussy, I grab her ass and pull her to the edge of the washer. She wraps her legs around me so my hard cock is pressed against her, our clothing acting as a sensual barrier as I continue to squeeze and pull on her nipples.

"You've got me so hot," she whimpers, her hands sneaking lower as she pulls at the band of my sweats.

Pulling out my wallet and keys, I place them on the

washer beside us before taking off my sweats and briefs, kicking them to the side.

Her eyes remain transfixed as I take the condom out of my wallet and open up the package. "Wait!" she cries just before I slip it on.

Grabbing my cock with her small hand, she stares at it lustfully. "This has got to be the sexiest cock I've ever seen." She looks up and growls, "I *need* this inside me."

While I wholeheartedly agree, I take my time. I'm not some average teenage boy who can't control himself. Although this is just a quickie, I plan to surpass her fantasies.

"Show me your pussy," I tell her as I stroke my cock.

Her eyes light up as she pulls her panties to the side to show off her dark patch of pubic hair and that pink clit glistening with her excitement.

"I'd like to watch you play with yourself."

"You're so naughty," she purrs as her fingers sensuously begin rubbing her clit.

I love watching her tease herself, but it doesn't take long before my libido demands the tight caress of her pussy. I roll the condom down over my cock, needing to take her. Ripping off her panties, I coat my sheathed cock in her wetness before positioning it against her opening.

She whimpers sweetly in anticipation as I slowly push myself inside her.

*Fuck...*

There is nothing hotter than watching my cock disappear inside a woman. This girl may have a tiny figure, but her pussy eagerly conforms to my shaft. I pull out for the sheer pleasure of watching it disappear inside her again.

She looks up at me and pleads, "I want you to fuck me hard, so fucking hard I scream."

Knowing she likes her nipples pinched, I plan to give her exactly what she's asking for. However, I'd prefer us not getting caught in the act.

Using what I have on hand, I wad her panties into a ball. I can tell by the excitement in her eyes that it turns her on when I stuff those wet panties in her mouth.

My level of control quickly erodes as I start thrusting into her while I listen to her muffled screams of pleasure fill the air. Determined to make it last as long as possible, I fuck her deep, then stop for several seconds before starting up again.

She looks up at me, her dark eyes burning with desire as I begin pounding her harder. Wanting to see how much she can take, I grab onto her hips and thrust even deeper.

Her passionate screams suddenly go silent and her whole body begins shaking. I feel her pussy squeezing my cock hard as a gush of liquid comes out.

I look down in surprise to see a puddle of clear liquid on the floor.

She takes the panties from her mouth and tells me, "I only do that when I get fucked really hard." Looking down between her legs, she adds, "I don't know why it happens, but it feels fucking fantastic!"

Although I have no idea what's going on, I know one thing—she likes it and I don't want to stop. Grasping her hips again, I tell her, "No holding back."

Her eyes grow wide as I reposition myself to take her again. She stuffs her mouth with her panties and grabs onto my wrists. Looking as if she's a cowboy preparing for an intense bull ride, she nods to me, indicating she's ready for the ride to begin.

I grit my teeth as I begin rolling my hips, taking her as deeply as I can. She begins moaning into her lace panties as she takes the challenge of my cock. When I feel her body starting to relax, I change the rhythm and begin thrusting into her hard.

She moans loudly.

Knowing what she's waiting for, I grab her waist tighter and begin pumping her like a jackhammer. This time, I have no plans to stop until I'm coming deep inside of her quivering pussy.

I give into the intense sensation as my climax builds. When I feel her body start to shake again, I know she is close. The moment I feel the gush of her wetness, I lose all control.

It takes everything in me not to cry out in passion as I find release. When I pull out, I have to steady myself because of the intensity of the orgasm.

I look down at the floor and see it is covered with more of the clear liquid from her unusual orgasms.

I take the panties from her mouth. "Hard enough for you?"

She throws her head back, her chest flushed from her multiple orgasms and grins. "So fucking hard…"

# Comrade

On Monday, I'm ready and waiting for the Russian in my Molecular Biology class. After studying basic phrases, my plan is to establish a lab routine equitable to both of us. I refuse to carry him through the entire course.

I watch the door, waiting for Durov to appear, expecting the same boisterous entrance as last time, but I am sorely disappointed.

He never shows.

After class, I wait to speak to Dr. Barr and ask if he has dropped the class, but she informs me he's still registered.

Annoyed, I throw my Russian dictionary back in my backpack, convinced I have been saddled with a slacker.

I walk out of class, trying to reign in my anger, but scream in frustration, "Damn it to hell!" once I make it out of the building.

A group of students walking by elbow each other and laugh as they pass me. Normally not one to lose control like that, I'm now resenting the Russian even more.

Needing to divorce myself from my current mood, I pull out the Nikon camera I bought over the weekend and go in search of a subject to photograph. It surprises me how looking at the world through a camera lens makes you see everyday objects in a different light.

Walking around the campus, I'm suddenly aware of random sculptures I've failed to notice before, as well as the detailed architecture of the older buildings. In trying to get an unusual angle for one of my shots, I inadvertently capture someone in my frame. The person has chosen a particularly secluded spot and curiosity gets the better of me.

Focusing my lens, I take a picture before realizing it's the Russian. The look of utter devastation on his face turns my blood cold.

I set the camera down, all anger toward him immediately evaporating.

I wonder what's happened and lift my camera again, watching silently as he stares at a single lit candle he's brought with him, mumbling words only he knows while tears run down his face.

Although he doesn't know it yet, I relate to the pain radiating from him even from this distance. It bonds me to the Russian in ways I don't understand.

I put my camera away and quietly leave him, not wanting to disturb such an extremely private moment.

I'm unsure if I will be able to break through the language barrier between us to discover the nature of the terrible burden he carries, but I am determined to support him in whatever way I can.

No one should be left to suffer alone.

I go to my lab the next day, not expecting to have a partner to work with. I've already decided to do the extra work necessary to keep Durov caught up. Settling in for a long session on my own, I'm surprised when he waltzes through the door, laughing loudly.

I stare at him, unable to reconcile what I'd witnessed yesterday with this carefree attitude he seems to be displaying now.

Still concerned for the guy, I ask if he is okay. "*Ty v poryadke?*"

He looks surprised, asking in Russian if I know his language.

"*Nyet.*" I pull out the three language books I've been studying over the last week.

He looks them over, his smile growing wider. "*Vy izuchayete russkiy yazyk dlya menya?*"

I look up the words to find he is asking if I am studying Russian for him. "*Da.*"

The breath is literally knocked out of me when Durov hits me on the back, shouting, "*Otlichno!*"

Unfamiliar with the word, I have to flip through the pages of my translation book to discover it means "very good".

I smirk at him and suggest, in Russian, that he return the favor by learning *my* native language.

Durov only laughs.

Picking up the lab notes, he hands them to me with an expectant look. I shake my head as I start reading through them. Even though I'm struggling to translate the notes, and know I'm going to end up staying longer than my classmates tonight, I'm glad the stubborn Russian is here.

Unfortunately, the long lab hours prevent me from picking up my photos that day, forcing me to rush to pick them up before Friday's class.

Not wanting to be late to my photography lecture, I have no time to look over the pictures I've taken. When Professor Brooks asks me to show her my work, I pull out the stack of photos and shuffle through them, trying to find the one I took at an odd angle.

I pull it out, setting the others on the desk, and hand it to her.

She looks at the photo critically for several seconds, then frowns slightly. "Is this really the one you wanted to show me, Mr. Davis?"

I see I've disappointed her and quickly shuffle though the others in the stack, but I know they aren't any better.

She sifts through them herself, and selects the candid shot I took of Durov. I never meant for anyone to see it, but I'm unable to snatch it back from her in time.

"Now *this* is an excellent example of the profound power photography can have," she states excitedly, turning to face the class. "Our ability to capture raw emotion on film is a priceless gift to humanity."

I glance at the picture of Durov and am struck again

by the agony I see reflected in his face. Needing to preserve his privacy, I explain to her, "I didn't take that picture as part of the class assignment. It's personal."

I can see the disappointment on her face when I take the photo back before she can show it to the other students. Tucking it back into the envelope, I slip it into my breast pocket.

Professor Brooks looks down at the initial photo I gave her. "It is a fine photo, Davis, but it lacks originality." She points to the one in my pocket. "But that one speaks volumes about the person who snapped it. Only *you* could have taken that photo. Remember that."

Walking over to Samantha, she turns back to me for a moment. "Truly powerful, Mr. Davis."

I see that Samantha has taken a photo of a crushed flower beside a crumpled gum wrapper and a flattened soda can.

"What are you trying to convey with this photo, Miss Clark?"

She frowns slightly as she stares down at her own work. "Originally, I was attempting to contrast the beauty of nature amongst the litter on campus. But, in the midst of getting the shot, a fellow classmate took it upon himself to purposely step on the flower I was photographing. Rather than fight it, I decided it was fitting so I call this one 'The Destructive Force of Man'."

Professor Brooks chuckles. "Poignant and resourceful. I want you to harness that artistic spirit." Looking back at the photo, she says, "I see real potential here."

Clark smiles to herself after Professor Brooks moves on. She has every right to be proud. I'm impressed by the photo, as well as the story behind it.

"An exceptional shot," I tell her.

She turns to me and nods stiffly, obviously pleased by my compliment.

After class, I pull out the photo of Durov again. It is so painful to look at, I find myself quickly returning it to my pocket. I feel badly for taking it without his permission, and even worse now, knowing another person has seen it.

Making the decision to give the photo to the Russian, I head straight to his dorm.

I find him in the dorm commons, sitting with a bunch of other guys around a large TV, watching reruns of *Saturday Night Live*. He is laughing louder than all those around him, which I find amusing, since he doesn't understand a word of it.

"Durov!" I call out.

He turns and breaks out in a grin when he sees me, waving me over to join him.

I shake my head and make a gesture toward the door. He shrugs, slapping the hands of several guys as he heads toward me.

I hate having to confess that I invaded his privacy by taking the picture. While I could destroy the evidence, Professor Brooks is right about the photo having power. I feel strongly that he should be the one to decide what becomes of it, even though I'm afraid of how the Russian will react.

Knowing how I would feel if the situation were reversed, I steel myself to face the consequences—whatever they may be.

I pull the photo out of my pocket and hand it to him. Durov glances at it and frowns.

He stares at me, waiting for an explanation.

I show him my camera and take out the stack of photos I took the same day, including the building I was photographing when I took the picture of him. I explain in simple terms that I was doing an assignment, then apologize for taking this one of him.

He stares at the photo again, but I cannot read the expression on his face.

I feel it is my duty to tell him my professor saw it. With extreme difficulty, I explain in Russian that Professor Brooks wanted to use it as a class example, but I am giving it to him instead.

He nods, smiling down at it. With a thick Russian accent, he says with pride, "So, she thinks I'm exceptional."

My jaw drops. "Wait…you speak English?"

Durov raises an eyebrow. "Possibly."

"You motherfucker!"

He shrugs, holding up the photo. "I'm not the one taking stalker photos of a man in mourning, comrade."

"Why in the hell have you been pretending you can't speak English?"

He shrugs nonchalantly. "It lets me know who my friends are."

While I can see the brilliance behind his scheme, after all the hours I've spent studying Russian, I want to fucking strangle the man.

Durov laughs when he sees the murderous look in my eyes. "So, tell me, Davis. Why did you take this photo?" he asks, waving it in front of my face.

I hesitate for a moment before choosing to be honest with him. "I saw something in you I recognized in myself."

He looks at the photo again. The smirk slowly leaves his face and is replaced with a look of pain. Putting his hand on my shoulder, he says in a solemn voice, "I'm sorry to hear that."

"What happened to you?" I ask, looking down at the picture.

He shakes his head, growling hoarsely. "I can't speak of it...not yet. You?"

I stare up at him, debating if I should reveal the truth. Choosing to follow my gut, I tell him, "I lost someone close through suicide."

I hear his sharp intake of breath before he abruptly turns away from me.

He shakes his head several times violently. The photo falls to the ground as he walks away in silence.

Durov's reaction confirms my suspicions, leaving me to wonder who he has lost.

# Breaking My Defense

Picking up the photo from the ground, I return it to my pocket for safekeeping. Finding myself alone after finally voicing what happened out loud leaves me suffocating with a grief I can't escape.

Even though it's been two years, it feels like yesterday since I lost him.

I quickly head to my dorm, needing to isolate myself as the images overtake me—all that blood, his haunting last breath, and the extinguishing of the light in his eyes...

Ignoring the people I pass, I rush to my room and slam the door shut as if it can save me from my own thoughts. Hitting my temples with my fists, I command the images to stop, unwilling to relive my last moments with him.

"*Papà...*" I cry out in anguish.

It feels as if my heart is being physically ripped open, and I fall to the floor, rocking back and forth as my father stares at me, unable to speak.

I can't reconcile his death—there's no way to wrap my head around it.

So, I do as I have always done, and force myself to stand up. I walk over to my desk, and take out my math book, picking out another equation from the back of the book.

By the time Anderson arrives, I am deep into a mathematic rabbit hole of my own making.

"Whoa…" he says as soon as he enters the room. "What's wrong, Davis?"

I barely look his way, mumbling, "Nothing."

"Bullshit! This entire room feels different—and it's coming from you."

"Leave it alone," I growl in warning, having just regained control over my emotions.

Anderson strides over and sits on my bed beside me, something he's never done. "Look, I've been on the ranch all of my life. I can tell when an animal is suffering."

I give him a sideways glare. "You calling me an animal?"

He shakes his head. "All I'm saying is that I can tell you're suffering and it's eating you alive."

When he puts his hand on my shoulder, I flinch.

"What happened today?"

"Nothing happened. It's just a bad memory I'm trying to forget."

"Does it have to do with your family?"

I close my eyes, the entirety of my father's death playing out in my mind. I can't stop it, and a sob escapes my lips.

Anderson places his broad hand on my shoulder. "I'm here for you, buddy."

I've talked to therapists until I was blue in the face, but I've never found solace or comfort in voicing what happened out loud—I've actually found the opposite to be true.

I purposely turn from him, an angry ball of sorrow, refusing to talk.

Anderson says nothing, but the pressure of his hand remains on my back. For some reason, I find his physical presence oddly soothing. Despite having such a muscular stature, Anderson has a gentleness about him so that his steadfastness comforts rather than challenges me.

I eventually glance at the clock and realize an hour has passed. The bastard is still with me, not saying a word, but not leaving, either. It is his perseverance that ultimately wins over my confidence, and I finally open up to him.

"I don't have a family, Anderson." That cold fact hangs in the air, choking me with its weight.

"I have extended family, certainly, but the people who raised me no longer exist and it eats at me." I mull it over before I share with him, "I'm convinced if my father had died in an accident, or even from a heart attack, I would have been able to get past this. But that's not what happened."

I look into Anderson's eyes, drawing from his strength as I build up the courage to expose my deepest pain.

"My father died in my arms when I was fifteen...after shooting himself in the head."

"Holy fuck," Anderson responds, the look of shock on his face letting me know he still has no idea who my father is...*was*.

"I still can't accept the fact that he's gone. I expect him to show up at any minute, apologizing for his absence. I know it's stupid—but I still hope to see him walking through the door."

Anderson shakes his head. "Not stupid at all."

I laugh sarcastically. "I know better. There's no need to sugarcoat it."

"Are you kidding? If my dad died, you can fucking bet I'd be on my knees daily, begging God to bring him back."

Trying to explain what it feels like, I tell him, "The pain of his death remains with me like a fifty-pound anchor crushing my chest every second of every day. It never lets up, and the weight of it only serves to remind me of how much I've lost."

My words spur Anderson to ask the one question I dread to hear.

"What about your mother?"

I have to swallow down the burning rage I feel, and answer him in a detached voice, "My mother died years before my father killed himself."

Anderson's jaw drops. "I've never understood how life could be so cruel to some people."

I give him a half-smile to hide the fact it feels as if I have ice in my veins. "There are times I've wondered if I am cursed."

"You can't let yourself think that way. Never allow it to enter your thoughts, Davis. The biggest obstacles we face are the limitations we place on ourselves."

His seemingly unshakeable confidence challenges me, and I ask, "How can you be sure?"

"I've learned it the hard way—on the back of a bull."

"A bull…" I can't fathom what would cause a person to ride a one-and-a-half-ton mass of angry muscle.

"I spent time in the hospital because of it, too," Anderson continues. "But in the end, it was my fault. I decided I was too young to take Crusher on. That thought alone spelled my doom. If I hadn't allowed that single, insidious thought to take over just before they opened the gate—that vital moment when my thighs were clenched around Crusher's churning mass of power—I would have won the national high school rodeo. I'm convinced of it."

"I agree with you that we make our own destiny. It's the only reason I came to college. Still, I harbor one doubt."

"What's that?"

"No matter how determined you are, it's still possible for fate to conspire against you."

Anderson nods. "But you can't give up. The instant you do, you lose."

"So, what happens when you have no more fight left?" I ask in a tired voice.

He flashes a smile, smacking me on the back. "You let your friends jump in the ring to take your place."

I frown, thinking to myself, *If only it were that easy.*

"Look, I have no idea what it's like to lose both parents—I don't even want to imagine it. But I *do* know what it's like to have a family who has my back. I may not be related to you, but I'd stand up and fight in your stead."

Looking at the sincerity in his eyes, I believe he would.

I instantly think of Durov, alone and in pain. There's no question I'd fight for him the same way.

I'm struck by a new thought. For years, I've been mourning the family I lost and will never get back. While it's a sad reality, I see now that I have the power to create something different and more permanent.

Looking at Anderson, a deep sense of gratitude hits me in the chest. I'm not an easy person to like. I stopped trusting everyone after my father's suicide, and refused to let people get close to me since his death.

Somehow, this bullwhip-wielding cowboy from Greeley has the determination and pure stubbornness to chip away at my defenses. "I don't know exactly how you did it, but you managed to take me away from the precipice I was teetering on today. A feat even my therapists could not achieve." I tell him with sincerity, "Thank you, my friend."

Anderson's face lights up. "Now, I just need to get you away from the textbooks so you can start living life again."

I snort with amusement. "No, it's the other way around. You need to start sticking your nose in books so the time you spend here isn't wasted."

Anderson clicks his tongue. "You are a stubborn fuck."

"I can say the same about you."

He tips an imaginary hat at me. "I take that as a compliment, buddy."

# Whip It

A few days later, Anderson manages to tear me away from my studies with an offer to show me how to crack his whip.

Naturally, I refuse, but he's prepared and sweetens the pot by stating that he's struggling in one of his classes and could use some help. I believe he's telling the truth, since I rarely see the guy studying at his desk. Knowing he could easily waste this entire year, I agree to the lesson on one condition. "As soon as we're done, we head back here to work on your class assignment. That's the only way this is happening."

He agrees without argument. "Deal. I suggest you wear a loose t-shirt. It'll help with your range of motion."

I take his advice and change while he adds to his casual ensemble by donning cowboy boots and a black hat.

"Are you going out like that?"

"Absolutely," he answers with a cocky grin. "I'm still on the hunt."

Having promised to help him on that front, I'm obligated to let it slide, but that doesn't stop me from rolling my eyes as he tips his hat to every girl he passes.

Along with his miniature bullwhip, he's asked me to bring several apples. I happen to be hungry and enjoy the tart bite of a ripe green apple, so I bring three. My stomach growls in anticipation as I carry them with me.

Anderson finds an open space in the grassy area of the outdoor commons which is lined with trees, It's far enough away from other students to assure that no one will walk into the path of the whip when he swings it.

"Stand back."

Anderson starts swinging his whip, but not in an aggressive manner. "I've got to get my muscles warmed up for this," he explains.

I nod, but my attention is focused more on the fruit than his actions because my stomach has started growling more loudly.

"Okay, give them to me," Anderson says, holding out his hand.

I do so reluctantly, but now he has my full attention as he tosses an apple into the air and swings his whip. It travels so fast, I don't even see it as it contacts with the fruit. A loud, explosive crack of this whip echoes across the campus as I watch the apple fall to the ground in two equal pieces. In rapid successions, the whip splits each apple cleanly in two, filling the air with its commanding sound.

Anderson turns toward me with a proud smirk. "What do you think of them apples?"

I look down at my snack in dismay, but I can't deny I'm impressed. "You've got real skill there."

The sound of his whip has drawn the attention of everyone around us, and they start gathering to see what is going on, chatting excitedly amongst themselves.

"Here," Anderson says, handing me the whip.

The girls start "oohing" and "ahhing" as he slowly strips off his shirt and hands it to one of them.

He takes the whip back from me. "It's important to introduce yourself to the whip. Feel her out, get to know her first before you begin manhandling her," he tells me solemnly as he winks at the girls.

I hear them sigh softly in response.

Damn, this guy knows how to ham it up.

I watch Anderson flick the bullwhip several times before he cocks his arm back and lets it fly. Everyone jumps when the crack explodes in the air, and giggles erupt from the girls.

Anderson looks at me with an "I told you so" expression.

I roll my eyes again, but my admiration for his whipping skills has definitely increased. He explains the basics of the whip and then hands it over to me, explaining how to hold it. "Don't grab it in the middle of the handle. That won't give you any leverage." He presses the end of it into my hand. "Wrap your fingers around it. That will give you control over the entire handle."

I am fully aware of everyone's eyes on me, and I have to trust that Anderson won't allow me to make a fool of myself.

He takes my arm and raises it over my shoulder. "You want to do it in a smooth, relaxed, up-and-down motion."

Anderson lets go of my arm and nods.

I take a deep breath, forgetting everyone around me. Taking his advice, I don't try to crack the whip immediately. Instead, I bring it up and down in a fluid motion several times to warm up.

I'm surprised that the whip feels as if it has a life of its own, and I look at Anderson in surprise.

He grins. "I see Myrtle likes you."

I don't know why his reassurance makes a difference, but it does. Ready to test her out, I stare straight ahead and take another deep breath.

I cock my hand back at a forty-five-degree angle and swing forward quickly, but no crack sounds.

"Excellent form," he compliments. "But if you want her to sing, you'll need to let the whip fully extend on the way up and let her fall behind you until the cracker is at its lowest point. That's when you bring your arm down, nice and straight. You don't want to go hitting yourself with the end of that whip. Trust me, even though she may look small, she can still rip an ear off."

I look down at the frayed-looking end of the whip, respectful of its power. There is an odd thrill, knowing I could hurt myself by simply swinging the whip. I ready myself again and cock my arm back, swinging it forward after the cracker falls behind me.

The satisfying crack caused by the whip makes me smile as people jump around me. I now understand why Anderson enjoys Myrtle so much...

After several more cracks of the whip, I relinquish its power, handing the bullwhip back to him.

He takes it with a glint in his eye. "Wanna see what

she can do?"

"Please."

Anderson tips his hat toward a group of women. "Ladies, you'll want to stand back for this."

He builds up the anticipation, slowly swinging the whip back and forth and side to side. When he is ready, Anderson nods to me with a grin.

I stare in wonder as his whip begins to dance, making music as it cuts through the air, the sequence of cracks creating its own exhilarating beat. I am seriously in awe as I watch him crack it at least eight different ways—over his head, behind him, and in rapid succession.

By the time he's done, the crowd is giving him enthusiastic and well-deserved applause, including myself.

He coils Myrtle up and walks over to me, placing his hand on my shoulder. "Let's head back to the dorm like I promised."

We walk through the wall of people, some of whom pat Anderson on the back, praising him for the performance. He obviously enjoys the attention, based on the charming grin on his face.

I, on the other hand, do not care for it and keep my head down.

"Handsome stranger!"

I look up to see the girl I had a tryst with in the laundry room standing in the middle of the crowd. I smile at her as we walk past, grateful to see her again. For some unknown reason, I haven't run across her since that day we bumped into each other in the laundry room, and I've wondered if she was still around.

Anderson and I finally free ourselves from his many admirers and start on our way back to the dorm. We're both startled when someone comes up behind and grabs Anderson's hat.

"Hey!" he complains, trying to snatch it back.

I turn to see Durov place the cowboy hat on his head and grin at us. "I saw what you were doing back there..." Anderson makes a swipe for his hat, but the Russian is too fast. "I didn't know you were a keeper of cows."

"Very funny." Anderson grumbles, successfully getting the hat back from him on his second attempt.

"I must admit, American cowboy, I'm impressed," Durov states.

Anderson shrugs. "Just something I picked up as a boy."

"Don't be so modest."

Durov turns to me. "And, you, comrade. You wish to master the bullwhip as well?"

"No. Anderson simply wanted to show me what it can do."

"I'd be happy to teach you, buddy," Anderson tells me.

"Do you only whip cows with it?" Durov asks.

Anderson laughs. "I don't whip them. I herd the cattle with it."

"Shame," Durov states sadly.

"However, I could be persuaded to whip a certain Russian, if you're so inclined."

Durov smirks at Anderson. "I am not, but I know some who are."

Anderson looks at him as if he's crazy—and maybe he is. But I'm relieved to see the Russian. He missed our last Biology class, and I was concerned enough to go searching for him after, but I never found him.

Durov leans over to me and whispers, "You know that picture you took?"

"Yes, I have it locked in my desk. Do you want it?"

"I want you to give it to your professor with my blessing. There is beauty in pain—I understand that. Since she admired the photo, I want her to have it."

I look at him in shock. "Is that truly what you want?"

"It is."

I would hate to have my emotions exposed like that, but Durov is an enigma, unlike anyone I've ever met.

Durov flicks Anderson's hat to get his attention. "I especially liked your Volley Crack."

Anderson's annoyance at having his hat messed with is quickly replaced with interest. "So you know about bullwhips, do ya?"

"Only through observation."

Anderson stands back to look at him. "You don't strike me as the type of guy who spends time on a ranch."

Durov chuckles. "You are correct. I am not."

"Then do you mind explaining how you're familiar with bullwhips?"

The Russian's smile broadens. "I may tell you…someday."

He leaves us, striding away confidently as if he owns the world.

"Your friend is odd," Anderson states.

I agree, with a sense of pride.

# Fun in the Sun

With fall semester finals looming, I have been studying particularly hard. If I ace these classes, and follow it up in the spring, there is a strong possibility I'll be able to advance a full year.

I know Anderson is focused on enjoying his time here, but I need to get out as quickly as possible and begin my adult life. I won't be free until I am financially independent. I'm thankful to my uncle and aunt for funding my college tuition, but I loathe owing anyone—especially family.

This feels like purgatory to me.

Until I've paid them back and am earning my own way, I will be vulnerable. I'll do whatever it takes to sever all ties to my past.

However, I can tell Anderson is getting nervous about our bet when he asks, "Hey there, buddy, I was thinking... Why don't we enjoy a day relaxing on the beach?""

I look up from my desk. "Not interested."

"Life's so much more than books and endless tests, young grasshopper, but how can you know this when you spend your days stuck in this room? It's time to live a little."

"That is exactly what I *am* doing," I correct him. "I plan to graduate early through sheer will and effort so I can begin my life."

Anderson shakes his head in disbelief. "You're missing the whole point. This *is* your life—right now. You're a young man living on a campus of possibilities, my friend, and it's my solemn duty to open your eyes to what you've been missing."

I put my arm around him in a fatherly manner. "And it's my duty to help you realize that life is not all fun and games. What's the point of going to college and acquiring tuition debt if you aren't going to seriously apply yourself every day you're here?"

Anderson frowns and the light seems to leave the room. When I meet his harsh gaze, I regret my words.

Just when I think he's about to explode with pent-up anger, he lets out a howl of laughter. "You're one insulting little bastard, Davis. No wonder you don't have many friends."

I chuckle at his insult. "As much as I appreciate your need to *fix* me, I'm content to remain in this room, focused on my schoolwork. Go enjoy your day on the beach."

I return to my book, legitimately fascinated by Dr. Bruce Dunn's revolutionary work on the power of the mind.

Anderson slams the textbook shut.

"What the hell, man?" I shout.

"All work and no play make Davis an extremely dull boy," Anderson answers with an impudent grin.

"Fuck you." When I go to open the book again, he takes it from me. "Nope. You're coming with me today."

"Like hell I am."

"I'm headed to the ocean for some sun, and your pasty white skin is in some serious need of some," he says, covering his eyes as if the glare from it hurts.

"Very funny. Now give me back the damn book."

Anderson's grin only grows bigger. "Only way you're reading this book today is if you're on the beach."

I let out an irritated sigh.

"You're in freaking California! You should *not* spend all your waking days stuck here on campus. It's not right!"

"I don't have swim trunks or even a beach towel," I tell him. Despite my protests, I know he's right. I've become a hermit.

"I'm positive they sell that shit at the beach," he laughs.

"I'm not interested in being gone all day."

His eyes light up, knowing he's won. "I wouldn't dream of keeping you away that long."

I don't believe Anderson for a second, but simply mentioning the beach has me thinking back to those days in Italy with my father, and I'm suddenly home-sick—needing to feel the ocean breeze against my face.

Still, I warn him, "You're going to owe me for this."

"Owe you?" Anderson scoffs. "For taking you to the beach?"

I nod slowly.

After a few seconds, he shrugs. "Fine, I owe you then."

He borrows a friend's car to drive us to Hermosa Beach, and I have to admit that when we crest the final hill and look down at the expansive blue waters stretching out to the horizon, I actually catch my breath.

I'd forgotten how much my soul connects with the ocean.

"You doing okay there, buddy?" Anderson asks, noticing the change in me.

I turn to him, trying to underscore my excitement. "This might not have been a bad idea, after all."

His boisterous laughter fills the car. Grinning, he gives me a hard sock in the arm. "I'm going to win that bet, Davis. Just you wait and see."

I *knew* he was motivated by the bet. Anderson is going to lose, but believes today's outing will hinder my focus. I'm not so gullible, but...why not pretend that I am?

I smile at him.

*Sure hope you're ready for Calculus next year.*

Finding a parking lot at the beach proves to be a challenge, but we finally secure a spot and head down to the pier.

Tourist shops line the streets on both sides. Stopping at a random one, Anderson walks in and tells the beautiful woman who works behind the counter, "Any recommendations on swim trunks for this guy? He can't be trusted to look trendy without help."

She appears to be in her early twenties, sporting a

copper tan and long platinum blonde hair that complements her skin tone. She looks me over, batting her eyes
flirtatiously. "I'm sure your friend would look good in
anything he wears."

I wink at her before giving Anderson a self-satisfied
smirk.

He grins, offering her a challenge. "Impress me with
your suggestion."

She moves from behind the counter, walking over to
the row of hanging swimwear. Flipping through the
hangers, she pulls one out with neon pinks and greens
and holds it up to me.

"Sorry, not my style," I inform her.

"No problem," she replies, putting it back.

While she continues looking, Anderson nudges me.
"I'll grab a couple of beach towels while you shop."

After several additional offerings, she comes up with
a gray one with a sunset motif.

"Yes. That will do."

"He'll need some footwear, as well," Anderson calls
from the back of the store.

"Are you interested in leather sandals?" she asks.

I chuckle, shaking my head. "No, a simple pair of
flip-flops will do. I don't plan on staying long."

She twirls her hair, tilting her head in a flirtatious
manner. "That's a shame."

"Got any Frisbees or hacky sacks, beautiful?" Anderson asks, walking up to her.

She stares at him, blushing an even deeper shade of
red. "Sure…um…that second row…no, third…to your
left…no, right."

Anderson winks at her. "Awesome."

He glances at me when she's not looking, giving me a roguish grin. Yeah, he's all too aware of the affect he has on women and, unlike me, he embraces it without a shred of restraint.

After I pay for my items, he tells me to change in the back while he purchases the towels.

Since I don't relish the idea of undressing inside a tiny bathroom stall at the beach, I appreciate the suggestion. I shed my pants and underwear and slip on the swim trucks, replacing my shoes with the cheap flip-flops, and throw everything in the shopping bag, but I purposely keep my t-shirt on.

When I come out, however, I see that Anderson has not only taken his t-shirt off, but is flexing his muscles for the clerk. She seems completely enamored and doesn't notice when I approach.

"Are you ready, Casanova?" I ask drolly.

He chuckles as he leans on the counter and tells her, "If you get a break, be sure to join us on the beach."

I clear my throat. "We're not planning on staying long."

Anderson smacks me on the back. "You need some color, man, and that takes time." He turns to her and says, "Poor soul has been cooped up in his dorm room for so long, he's lost all his Italian coloring."

"You're Italian?" she asks me in a dreamy voice.

I want to avoid anything associated with my father that could lead to my identity, so I answer, "I'm just a typical American mutt with a variety of nationalities mixed in."

She smiles invitingly. "I like mutts…"

I chuckle. "Good to know."

"I'm off to introduce Davis to the sun," Anderson announces. He looks back at her as we leave and adds, "Keep us in mind if you get that break, beautiful."

I shake my head as we walk out and head down to the pier. "You're really incorrigible."

"What? Because I love women?"

"I enjoy them, too, but you don't see me flirting every second of every day."

"That's because you've got your priorities wrong. Women are far more interesting than books."

"Books win over people every time, no question."

"And that is what sets us apart, but I aim to change that…starting today."

We find an empty spot on the beach and Anderson hands me a towel as he sets his down on the sand and lays on it, hands crossed behind his head. "Man, I could get used to doing this every day."

I go to lay my towel down and snort when I see what's printed on it. He's given me a white towel with a rainbow and prancing unicorn in the middle. "Good God."

Anderson snickers to himself as he puts his shades on. "No need to thank me, buddy."

I glance around and see a little girl eyeing the towel, so I toss it to her saying, "It's yours to keep."

"Thank you!" she exclaims excitedly, smashing it against her chest.

I turn back to the ocean, captivated by the power of it. Pulling off my t-shirt, I ball it up to use as a headrest and lay directly on the sand. The warmth of the sand relaxes me as I give into the soothing sounds of the rolling waves hitting the shore, enjoying the ocean breeze caressing my skin as I lie there.

Damn, I'd forgotten how good it felt.

A random vision floats by…a day on the beach making sandcastles with my father.

*I miss you, Papà.*

The thought catches me off guard and I immediately bury it.

I can't afford to think like that, because dealing with that untapped pain would completely derail my efforts at school.

I open my eyes and look up as a thin cloud drifts by above me. I reset my way of thinking, forcing myself back to this moment rather than dwelling on the thoughts in my head.

Pushing my toes into the sand, I revel in the feel of each tiny grain. The sound of the ocean waves crashing against the shore calls to me like a childhood friend. It's been a long time since I've felt the waves carry me along, and I find I can't resist the urge to join them.

"Come on," I command as I stand up.

"Where are you headed?" Anderson asks.

"You can't come all the way to the ocean and not jump in."

"Hey, I just came to soak in the rays."

"You're going to soak, all right," I tell him, holding out my hand to him.

Anderson removes his sunglasses and takes hold of my hand, but as soon as he stands up, he pushes me to the ground. "Last one to the water buys lunch."

"Cheater!" I yell after him, getting up and running. As soon as we're in deep enough, I jump onto his shoulders and dunk him thoroughly.

He comes sputtering up out of the water and then lunges at me. What he doesn't know is that I am an excellent swimmer and have no problem outmaneuvering him.

"Seems cowboys aren't good swimmers," I laugh.

"Laugh all you want, pasty boy. At least I got you out in the sun."

I swim closer, wanting him to think he has a chance of getting even. But, just as he lunges, I change direction. As he hits the water, I jump on his back and dunk him again. I can't stop laughing when he tries to stand up and is hit by a rogue wave that sends him straight into the sand.

Anderson gives me an irritated smirk. "Yuck it up, buttercup."

When I finally stop laughing, I tell him, "I haven't had this much fun since...oh, hell, I don't know when."

"Hey, isn't that the girl from the store?" Anderson says, pointing to the shore.

Sure enough, I see the girl searching for us on the beach.

I should have known it was coming. One second of distraction and my face hits the water as Anderson crashes on top of me.

This time, I'm the one breaking the surface, coughing and sputtering. Naturally, all I hear is the sound of Anderson's howling laughter.

I dunk my head back in the water momentarily, then brush back my hair. Heading to the shore, I ignore him as I start toward the girl *way* ahead of him.

# My First

When I see the woman turn away, I whistle loudly to catch her attention. She glances back in my direction and waves when she sees me.

I look at Anderson and give him a nod. He may have gotten me under the water, but I'm going to be the one who gets to the girl first.

"Don't forget—you still owe me a lunch," he yells behind me, struggling to catch up.

As if on cue, the blonde smiles as she presents a picnic basket to me. "I thought it would be nice to have lunch together."

I guess I won't be owing Anderson anything.

"Sounds great. When do you have to get back to work?" I ask her, impressed that she's managed to come.

"Actually, my parents own a place here on the beach. I just work at Eddy's to pass the time whenever I watch their house. When I got the invite to join you, I immediately called in my replacement."

Anderson comes up behind me, dripping wet. "Well,

hello there, beautiful."

She bites her lip, holding the basket up. "I made this for you guys."

"Well, now, aren't you a sweet thing?"

"It's not every day I'm invited to hang with two gorgeous men. Do you mind if I take a picture of you both?"

"Sure, but let me dry off first," he tells her. Anderson dries himself off slowly, making sure to emphasize every muscle as he goes. He makes quite the show of it and by the end I have to roll my eyes.

He tosses the wet towel at me, stating, "You can use mine, since you gave away the one I bought you, you ungrateful wretch."

The woman laughs, "I wondered who that towel was for."

I nod at the little girl lying on the unicorn towel. "Anderson bought it for her. He just didn't know it at the time."

"Anderson, is it?" she asks him. "And what's your first name?"

"Brad, darlin'."

Her smile widens. "Pleased to meet you, Brad. I'm Rhythm."

Uncertain I've heard her correctly, I repeat her name. "Rhythm, did you say?"

"Yes, my parents are musicians. My mother thought it was cute."

Even though it's irrational, I'm suddenly worried that her parents may have run in the same social circles as my father. However remote the possibility, if I can keep the attention focused on her, it won't have to become a topic of discussion.

I smile, telling her, "I find your name charming."

She blushes. "So, what's yours?"

"I go by my last name which happens to be Davis."

"Really, just Davis?" she asks.

Anderson smacks me on the back. "He thinks it gives him an edge with girls."

Rhythm looks at me with a flirtatious grin. "You might have something there. Makes you seem mysterious, Mr. Davis."

Anderson shakes his head at me, and mutters in disbelief, "And you say *I'm* incorrigible…"

Rhythm gets out her camera and asks us to stand with our backs to the ocean. Anderson rubs the top of my head, and I elbow him, brushing my hair back into place before I elbow him again.

"You two act more like brothers than friends," Rhythm giggles.

"Living in a dorm with this guy is no easy task," I tell her.

"I think it's the other way around, buddy," he laughs.

Anderson throws his arm around my shoulder as she takes the picture and whispers, "Tell me this isn't better than books."

Rhythm takes several more and tells us, "When I get the film developed, I'll be sure to make extra copies for you guys."

"I'll be sure to give you my address, darlin'," Anderson answers with a seductive grin.

I know he wants a picture so he can lord it over me

for the rest of the year—so be it.

"Would you two like to lunch at the beach house?" she asks, holding up her basket temptingly.

Anderson raises his eyebrows. "You have a beach house?"

"It's my parents. I take care of it whenever they travel on business."

"By all means," he answers with a charming grin, "let's go to the beach house!"

"I was hoping you would say that."

As we walk down the public path between the ocean and the row of expensive homes, I notice each one is unique, speaking to the owner's personal aesthetics.

Rhythm informs us, "We call this The Strand. It's the place to see and be seen."

"I can understand why you like it here," Anderson says, stopping at a large home covered in ornate carvings. "I've never seen anything like this."

I feel differently as I look at the row of houses and see the people partying inside. I like my privacy too much to be on display like that, but I have to admit the distinctive houses are interesting, and their view of the ocean is enviable.

Rhythm leads us to a two-story, Spanish-inspired home with a rose garden and waterfall in the small front yard. She opens the gate and invites us to join her. As we walk inside, I can feel the eyes of strangers on me as they slowly stroll past, and I suspect they are extremely jealous of us.

Opening the door, Rhythm invites us inside. Anderson whistles in appreciation once we step inside.

"This is one mighty fine pad you have here, darlin'."

"Eh," she replies, shrugging her shoulders. "I've grown up with it, so it fails to impress me. But I'm glad you like it." She then turns to me. "What about you, Davis? What do you think?"

"I agree it's impressive. However, I find you far more compelling."

"Oh…you're quite the charmer," she purrs.

Anderson glances at the basket hungrily and asks, "What do you have in that basket of yours, beautiful?"

She actually blushes when she opens it for him.

He peeks inside and breaks out in a grin. "I'm one hundred percent with you on this."

I'm surprised by his reaction. Peeking in the basket myself, I see she has a variety of condoms and a bottle of chocolate sauce. "Ah…"

She looks at me expectantly. I have never done a threesome and I'm not even sure how to proceed. I look to Anderson, who has a lustful glint in his eyes, wondering if he has experience in this area.

Regardless, I'm game.

In answer to her unspoken question, I lean down and kiss her on the lips. Rhythm lets out a soft sigh as I pull away.

My cock is now fully invested.

"Give me a minute to freshen up," she says, grinning at both of us as she climbs the stairs and disappearing into a room.

As soon as she shuts the door, I ask Anderson, "You do this kind of thing often?"

"Are you kidding? This is something I've only ever

dreamed about. You?"

"First time."

He chuckles. "So what's our plan of action?"

"We keep to opposites ends. I have no desire to get to know you intimately, no offense."

"None taken. I have no interest in that pasty white body of yours."

I take a deep breath as I hear her humming upstairs. "We're really going to do this…"

Anderson punches me in the arm. "Fuck yeah, we are."

Ten minutes later, Rhythm has yet to return, so I start exploring the main floor. The house faces the ocean with a spectacular view. I can't imagine how much the house must cost. Still, there is a constant stream of people walking by which I find disconcerting, so I go farther into the house where I find a study.

The walls of the room are covered in photos.

It's obvious that her parents are not only famous, but have traveled the world extensively, playing at different venues. I look at each photo, trying to determine where it was taken. Having traveled with my father when I was young, I'm familiar with many of the places I see in the photos.

I suck in my breath when I come across one with my father standing behind her parents in a large group. The picture was taken at a time when he was happy—when we were all happy. His candid smile stabs at my heart. He doesn't know what's coming…

I jump when Rhythm sneaks up behind me. Turning around, I see she's dressed in a simple silk robe, but her face and hair is done up like a professional model's.

"Quite the transformation," I comment.

She strikes a pose, pouting her lips sexily. "I figured I would go all out for you two."

What I keep to myself is that I preferred her casual look. However, knowing the effort she's put into her makeup, I see no reason to mention it.

Pointing to the picture, she says, "That one was taken somewhere in Europe. It was a huge event my parents did for charity, I think."

"It seems your parents travel a lot," I respond, purposely moving away from the photo. The fear of being exposed is nothing compared to the unexpected stab of pain I feel at seeing my father's smiling face.

Anderson enters the study and looks at all the photos on the walls. "Wow, when you said your parents were musicians, I had no idea they were famous. You're a celebrity, Rhythm."

"Celebrity by proxy is not the same. Not by a long shot," she tells him. "Everyone expected me to follow in their footsteps, especially with a name like mine." She sighs. "It's been a curse, really. While I appreciate listening to classical music, I have *zero* interest in playing it."

"What *are* you interested in?" I ask.

"I want to be a model, but the idea of that horrifies my parents."

"That's got to be rough, going against your parents' wishes," Anderson says, his voice tinged with sympathy.

"It is, but I'm not letting it stop me. I'm here selling tourist crap on the beach until my big break happens."

She smiles at me coyly. "So, what are your future aspirations, Davis?"

"I plan to graduate a year early so I can start a successful company and become financially independent."

"Admirable. I wish you lots and lots of success." She turns to Anderson. "And you?"

He only chuckles. "I haven't decided yet. But, like you, I'm *not* interested in following in my parents' footsteps."

"What do they do?"

"They're cattle ranchers in Colorado. My parents work damn hard, but I want more than what they have—struggling year to year with their survival dependent on the price of beef. Not me. I want my income to always match my level of output." He shrugs. "I just haven't decided what that looks like yet."

"Whatever you decide, you'll look good doing it," she tells him with a seductive grin. There's no denying Rhythm is hot as I stare at her pointed nipples pressing against that thin silk robe...

The atmosphere in the room becomes charged with sexual energy, but Anderson and I are unsure about how to proceed.

A problem solver by nature, I ask, "Rhythm, can you get me your camera? I'd like to get a couple shots of you."

Her eyes light up at the suggestion.

We follow her into the main room and I ask Anderson to shut the curtains. What we are about to do is X-rated, and we don't need the masses walking by looking in at us.

With the camera in hand, I start directing her, setting her in poses I find artistic but erotic. I tell Anderson to suggest a few himself, and Rhythm eats up the attention, eager to make our every vision a reality.

That's when I introduce the real reason I asked for the camera. "Anderson, why don't you join her? Hold her against you."

He gives me a nod of approval and strides over to Rhythm, taking her in his arms.

"Now, bend her over the couch and lift her robe up so we can get a sensual peek at her hot, little ass."

Anderson repositions her robe so it shows off her pink thong, which beautifully accents the roundness of her firm butt.

"Look back at me, Rhythm."

She lifts her head and turns toward me, smiling seductively.

"Damn you're hot, darlin'," Anderson tells her.

Her smile widens. Glancing at Anderson's crotch area, she can't help but notice the sizable hard-on growing in his swim trunks. Her eyes then drift between my legs and she bites her lip. "Why don't you put that camera down and you two boys join me on this couch?"

Rhythm grabs the chocolate sauce from her basket and lies back, drizzling it over her breasts. Anderson and I look at each other and smile as we sit down on either side of her.

Careful to leave each other plenty of room so we don't touch, the two of us descend on those delectable breasts, licking and sucking the chocolate off her until she's completely clean. Then we begin the real business of sucking and caressing her sumptuous tits.

Rhythm squirms and moans in pleasure, running her hands through our hair. "Oh, fuck yes…"

I seek out her lips, almost losing control when I hear her passionate moan as my tongue slips into her mouth. I'm turned on at the prospect of the two of us taking Rhythm at the same time because it's outside the realm of anything I've ever tried before.

As I continue to kiss her, I watch Anderson roll her hard nipple between his fingers. She reaches down and starts rubbing her hand against my swim trunks, teasing my cock. I'm so close to coming that my shaft is already dripping with precum.

I pull back and let Anderson kiss her while I tug lightly on her nipples before taking one into my mouth. I watch as her hand sneaks down to his swim trunks, but then she suddenly freezes.

Rhythm breaks the kiss, pulling on Anderson's trucks to get a look at his cock. For the first time, I see Anderson in all his glory. He hasn't been exaggerating about the size. It's truly massive.

Rhythm's eyes grow wide as she stares at his shaft. "Oh, my God…" she murmurs, trying to wrap her hand around it. "It's so *big*."

"All the better to please you with…" he growls, kissing her again.

I reach down between Rhythm's legs. A moan escapes her lips as I slide my finger under her thong. She twists her waist toward me and opens her legs wider.

Her shaved pussy has large outer lips that remind me of the soft petals of a flower. I start playing with her clit, coating her pussy with her own juices as she holds Anderson's large shaft tight in her grasp.

"Suck me," Anderson whispers hoarsely.

I sit back to watch as Rhythm tries to encase the large head of his shaft with her lips. His girth proves challenging, but her determination to take him deep is a turn-on for me. In response to her dedication, I slip my finger back into her, matching the rhythm of her mouth traveling up and down his cock.

She gets wetter as I begin to explore her pussy, searching for her G-spot. When I find it, her body shudders with excitement. I take my time, building up her climax as I try to regain control over my own libido.

When I get her past the point of no return, she cries against Anderson's cock, "Oh, fuck, I'm coming!" Her pussy starts contracting around my finger as she orgasms.

I look up at Anderson and smile. I enjoy a woman who comes easily.

Anderson readjusts Rhythm's position, pulling her over the arm of the couch so her back is arched. He gets down on the floor and spreads her legs wide. "You have fun with Davis while I eat you for lunch."

Rhythm purrs with excitement as I slip off my trunks and rejoin her on the couch. I hold my breath as she grasps my shaft, willing myself not to lose control because I'm so damn close.

"I must say, Mr. Davis, that is one handsome cock you have there." She kisses the head of my shaft before wrapping her lips around it. I can't prevent the groan that escapes.

"Oh, yeah, that's fucking hot," Anderson growls lustfully from between her legs. "Show me just how deep you can take him."

His head disappears between her thighs, and Rhythm begins whimpering excitedly as he goes down on her.

Pushing my cock deeper into her throat, Rhythm starts popping up and down on my shaft.

"Oh, fuck..." I groan again, as her throat tightens around my already sensitive cock. I grab onto her head to guide her movements, needing to slow her down.

The change in tempo not only helps me regain control, but it also enhances my enjoyment of her fellatio skills.

Rhythm suddenly stops and her body becomes rigid as she climaxes. "Oh, Brad...that tongue...that tongue!"

Rhythm eagerly grasps my cock again, sucking it enthusiastically as Anderson teases her clit. Apparently, he knows his way around a woman's pussy, because it doesn't take long for her to start moaning passionately on my cock again, her thighs trembling as he hits the perfect spot.

I can think of nothing I want more than to sink my shaft deep into her quivering pussy, so I turn her around so she's on all fours and move into position behind her. Grabbing a condom from her basket, I roll it onto my cock while Anderson stands up.

Rhythm props her arms on the couch so his shaft is level with her mouth, then smiles up at him as she grasps his huge rod in her two hands.

Anderson fists her hair as he guides her lips onto his cock. I watch Rhythm take that massive shaft into her mouth while I slowly penetrate her wet pussy.

She fills the room with her passionate moans.

I find the visual of her bobbing up and down his shaft incredibly erotic as I start to thrust into her. I give into the sensation, thoroughly embracing the kinkiness of what we are doing.

Two guys fucking one girl...I never imagined I'd be doing such a thing.

I start to pound her harder, liking the way her ass bounces with each thrust. Grabbing her buttocks, I thrust even deeper. Her pussy is so tight, I can feel her swollen G-spot. Taking advantage of that, I stroke it at just the right angle. It doesn't take long before she's screaming, begging me not to stop.

The moment her pussy starts pulsing with yet another orgasm, I climax, thrusting into her hard and fast.

"Suck me until I come," Anderson groans huskily. Even though her whole body is trembling from her multiple orgasms, Rhythm eagerly refocuses her attention on his cock. Unable to take all of him in her mouth, she uses her hand to stimulate his shaft while she concentrates on sucking the head of his cock.

It isn't long before his lusty grunts of satisfaction fill the air, and I watch as he comes in her mouth. Rhythm swallows it hungrily, licking up his remaining come after his climax is over.

Anderson collapses onto the couch next to us, sighing with contentment.

Rhythm turns her head toward him, wiping her lips. "Damn, I love having a big juicy cock for lunch."

He caresses her cheek. "And I definitely love watching you eat it, darlin'."

I say nothing as I watch the two, feeling completely satisfied in a way I never have before.

Anderson looks at me. "What are you thinking about over there, Davis?"

I'm not willing to admit what's really going through my head because I would never hear the end of it.

But, the truth is, this is *way* better than books.

# The Invitation

Despite the good times we've had on the beach, when finals hit, I seclude myself in my dorm room to ensure I earn the exemplary grades I need to move ahead next year.

Anderson can't believe I've slipped back into my old ways and insists I'm moving in the wrong direction.

"I'm just suggesting one night on the town. You've been cooped up here for weeks now. Missing one night of study isn't going to make or break you. I swear I see mushrooms growing out your butt."

I give him an irritated look. "If you were serious about college, you'd be cramming for that Physics class. You do realize you aren't going to magically pass that course?"

"Look, you promised you'd go out again, and it's been nearly three weeks. Rather than study harder, give that brain of yours a rest."

"No," I answer firmly, ending the discussion.

"It that really how this is going down?" he asks.

"I'm afraid so."

"Then you leave me no other choice."

Anderson walks out of the room in a huff, but I don't care. With him out all night, at least I won't be bothered. I slip on my headphones and get back to work.

A half an hour later, Anderson bursts into the room with Durov following behind him. Seriously? He brought the Russian in on this?

"Leave me alone, Durov," I growl angrily, not in the mood for his games.

Without warning, he physically grabs me and starts dragging me toward the door. "You're coming with me," the Russian insists, shoving me out into the hallway.

I stand up and straighten my clothes, unruffled. Nothing is going to deter me, including him. I state with disdain, "I have zero interest in getting drunk tonight."

Durov only laughs. "Trust me, comrade. I have something *far* more interesting in mind."

Something in his tone catches my attention.

I stare at him, noting a mischievous glint in his eye that seems to speak to something much bigger than a simple night on the town.

I look at Anderson. "You have got any idea what he's talking about?"

Anderson shrugs. "Not a clue. He won't say."

"I will only offer this opportunity once, comrade. After tonight, it will be closed to both of you forever," Durov tells me, his tone deadly serious.

"What kind of opportunity?" I demand, believing his secretiveness to be both unnecessary and childish.

Durov looks down the hall before he answers in a

low voice. "It's a chance to visit a private club I frequent. It will change your life. But I warn you, it is not for the faint of heart."

I have to admit he has my attention. However, if he expects me to sacrifice a full night of study, I need more details.

The Russian flatly refuses. "Either you trust me or you do not."

Trust is not something I give easily, but I respect Durov. Somehow, despite the fact that he spends far too much time flirting with women and drinking vodka on the sly, the little fucker still excels as a student. Unlike me, he doesn't have to devote hours to studying.

"Why pass up this once-in-a-lifetime opportunity, buddy?" Anderson asks. "It's not like your books are going anywhere."

I'm still not convinced. I look back into the room at the huge textbook sitting on my desk beside the piles and piles of notes.

For reasons I can't fathom, I suddenly feel a sense of exhilaration I haven't felt since I was a boy.

I've already made my decision to go, but as I look at Durov, I mutter, "Why do I have a feeling I will live to regret this?"

The Russian flashes a wicked grin. "If truly living for the first time in your life is a problem for you, then, yes, you *will* live to regret this night, comrade."

Anderson slaps me on the back. "Here's to having our minds expanded outside the realm of college tests."

As the three of us make our way through the campus, I suddenly realize what this is all about and stop cold. "Durov, your 'private club' wouldn't happen to be some kind of illicit drug den, would it?"

He bursts out laughing, attracting the attention of passersby.

"Let me assure you that my drug of choice is naturally produced. Although..." He looks me over critically. "...it may be too harsh for the likes of you."

Now he has my defenses up, so I insist, "I'm not squeamish, Durov." I nod over at Anderson. "Although, I can't speak for my roommate."

Anderson punches me in the arm. "Fuck you, Davis. If you're trying to call me a sissy, I've got a bullwhip I'd like you to meet."

Durov nods at Anderson. "It was actually your experience with the bullwhip that got you invited tonight."

"Wait. Don't tell me. You're part of a Russian cowboy club. Is that it? I'm not surprised to hear you Ruskies like to ride steers for fun on the weekends," Anderson jokes.

"I ride something, yes, and it often grunts and squeals with pain," Durov replies with a slight smirk.

Based on Durov's cryptic answer, I realize there's a dangerous element to him I haven't noticed until now.

Anderson frowns at me. "I don't know what kind of crazy shit you're getting us into, Davis."

"Me? You're the one who started this."

"Hey, Durov's your friend, not mine."

Durov grins. "You will both thank me once the evening is over. Trust me." Placing his hands around both our shoulders, he adds, "This is a solemn gift I offer to you. Whether you choose to pursue it or not is your choice, but I guarantee you'll be changed by what you experience tonight." He squeezes our shoulders in a painful, viselike grip before letting go—then laughs to himself.

Foolish or not, I'm now thoroughly intrigued and follow the Russian as he leads us to the shadier part of town, taking us down a labyrinth of dark alleys until we come to what looks like an abandoned warehouse.

There, he knocks on the door three times in quick succession.

A voice from behind the door asks, "What's the one truth?"

Durov answers, "All is fair in passion and pain."

The door opens, and the man gives Durov a curt nod, but he gives Anderson and me a look of intense distrust.

"These are my friends," Durov explains. "I spoke to the Dungeon Master about bringing them tonight."

The man doesn't acknowledge Durov's reply. However, he does open the door wider. Growling under his breath, he glares at both of us as we pass.

Durov seems unconcerned about the man's hostility toward us.

As we walk down the hallway, he explains, "Tonight you are here to observer." He then adds with a dangerous glint in his eye, "So keep your distance from the scenes—unless you want to get hurt."

As if on cue, I swear a woman screams somewhere below us. "What the hell is going on? Are people being tortured here?"

The Russian answers my question with a roguish

grin. "What some consider torture, others consider ecstasy."

I hesitate before descending a long flight of metal stairs. Just then, I hear the woman let out another tormented scream. Soon after, I clearly hear her cry, "Please Master, more! More…"

A chill goes through me as I put my hand out to stop Durov before he opens the door. "I have an eerie feeling I won't be able to look at you in the same light after this."

"*Da,*" Durov agrees. "Tonight, you will both be required to address me as *Rytsar.*"

"That's Russian 'knight'," I mutter to Anderson.

Turning to Durov, I shake my head, declaring, "You can't be serious."

Durov's expression suddenly becomes somber, as does the tenor of his voice. "I assure you, I am."

Anderson bumps my shoulder. "Knight…Asshole…it's all the same." He gives Durov an exaggerated bow. "So be it, Rytsar Durov."

We hear a commotion on the other side of the door. Several men cheer loudly as a lone girl cries out in pain after an extremely loud snap.

"What's happening to her?" I demand.

"There is only one way to find out, comrade," he answers, gesturing to the door.

The exhilaration I felt earlier increases as I reach for the handle. Durov claps me on the shoulder, stating proudly as the door slowly creaks open, "Welcome to my world…"

"Rytsar!" a young woman shouts excitedly from deep

within the large basement. She is bound, naked, to a pole set in the center of the immense room. It's obvious she's thrilled to see him, which seems odd considering her body is covered in angry red marks as if she's been hurt.

Durov leaves us, confidently striding over to the young woman. Grabbing a fistful of her hair, he pulls her head back and kisses her passionately.

Anderson and I remain rooted where we are, watching in stunned silence.

I glance around the warehouse basement. It is dank—made up of cold brick and cement flooring. Strange contraptions line the walls, with heavy chains hanging from the ceiling and wooden poles set throughout the room. Severe-looking men dressed in black leather, as well as a preponderance of naked women, populate the huge area.

"What the hell is this, Duro—Rytsar Durov?" I ask when he returns to us.

He gestures to the massive room. "This is a BDSM dungeon, comrade. Down here, we fulfill our darkest fantasies with those who hunger for our brand of ecstasy."

I watch in disbelief as a woman parades another, more petite, woman into the room from a separate entrance. The first woman is leading the second by a leash.

"Strip for your Master," the woman commands.

The girl immediately undresses in front of us and bows her head as she stands there naked as the leash is detached from her collar.

Durov takes over. "Lift your hands above your

head," he orders.

She obediently places her wrists into metal cuffs above her, not objecting when he secures the locks and jerks on the chain to make it taught. Observing her closely, I swear she has a look of adoration on her face.

Durov begins muttering words in Russian, speaking in a menacing tone as he circles the girl. As she watches him, the lust in her eyes becomes mixed with what looks to be fear.

I understand I'm about to witness something dark—something perverted—and yet, I cannot look away as Durov picks up an ominous, multi-tailed leather whip and swings it in the air.

That instrument of punishment has no business touching, much less striking the girl, and yet Durov laughs seductively as he begins lashing her with it.

Her cries fill the dark dungeon as he lets loose on her back.

My mouth goes dry as I watch. The idea of purposely causing someone else pain is a completely foreign concept to me, and it would be upsetting if it weren't for that devoted look in the girl's eyes every time he pauses between volleys.

Even as Durov delivers those demanding strikes, she breathlessly begs him for more, shuddering and moaning in pleasure. When he's finished, the Russian moves up behind her and reaches around to play with her pussy. The girl tilts her head upward as she cries out in desire, orgasming in front of us.

I never knew this kind of sexual power was possible—the idea of delivering pleasure with intense pain.

Glancing over at Anderson, I can tell the concept fascinates him, as well. Durov releases the girl from her bonds and gives her one last, lingering kiss before smacking her hard on the ass. She squeals in pleasure, giggling afterward.

"Clean up," he orders.

Durov then strides over to us with a self-assured look on his face. "What do you think, comrade?"

"I'm not quite sure what to thin—"

A scream of pure terror interrupts my answer. I immediately turn to see a woman bound, spread-eagle, on a wooden table. The man attending her is whipping her pubic area repeatedly with a different kind of leather whip.

Durov glances at her and says, "The girl is being grossly disobedient and must be punished for her willfulness."

I cannot allow such a thing to happen and move toward them to intervene, but Durov grabs my arm to stop me. "It is not your place."

"But he's hurting her!" I growl.

"Hurting her, yes. But *not* harming her, comrade. There is a difference."

Anderson is equally riled. "I'm with Davis on this one. We are witnessing blatant abuse and are *required* to stop it."

Durov shakes his head. "Each girl here comes of her own free will, knowing full well what will happen once she enters the dungeon." He gestures around the room. "These submissives want this. There is no need to feel sympathy for them. This is what they live for."

I shake my head as I watch welts rising on the woman's thighs. "Well, it fucking looks harmful to me."

"What you are witnessing is consensual play between two adults," he insists. "She understood she would be punished for disobeying her Master. She wanted to push him so he would punish her. Do you hear her calling her safeword? Every submissive has one. Unless she calls it, he has her permission to punish her however he sees fit."

"It's not right..." Anderson growls, responding to her desperate cries of pain.

Rytsar grins. "Ah, but it feels so right. I have played with submissives since my father first introduced me to BDSM when I was fifteen. I guarantee you, I understand women far better than either of you."

"And, you're saying they like this stuff?" Anderson asks incredulously.

"Many do, in fact. Imagine a woman laying down her will, allowing you to do whatever you wish to her body..."

"Well," Anderson says in a sarcastic tone, "if I had *my* way, the only beating I would be doing is slamming my gigantic cock into her."

The Russian raises an eyebrow as his gaze settles on the bulge between Anderson's legs. "There are plenty of women here who would beg you to challenge them with your asset."

I can see Anderson starting to warm to the idea.

"As far as your bullwhip goes, think about it. Isn't there a part of you that would like to lick a woman's body with the instrument as you watch her squirm in pleasure?"

Anderson glances around the room, staring at the girls in various states of arousal, and I see a new appreciation dawn in his eyes as he mulls over Durov's words.

The Russian puts his arm around my shoulder. "The power exchange between two souls is intoxicating, comrade. It is like a drug—nothing compares to it."

"I'm sorry, Durov. I could never whip a woman."

"Did you not hear me when I said you could do *whatever* you wished? You are in control." He stares at me with those piercing blue eyes and says in all seriousness, "You are full of tension—I can see it in your face—and it's holding you back in your studies. The best way to break your stress is to release it on a willing partner. Trust me."

I chuckle. "So, is that how you maintain your high grades?"

"*Da*," he answers without shame. "I am stress free thanks to the devotion of my subs. I can think straight because of it—unlike you."

The sub from earlier walks up to him with her eyes focused on the ground. She bows at Durov's feet. "How may I serve you, Rytsar?"

He looks at me and grins. "This is a virgin Dom. Introduce him to our world."

The girl doesn't miss a beat, looking up at him and answering with a confident smile, "Yes, Rytsar. It would be my pleasure."

She turns to me and bows. "What would you ask of me?"

# Glee

My heart starts racing. I'm unprepared for such responsibility as I look down at the submissive bowing at my feet.

Taking a deep breath, I take the girl's hand and help her back to her feet. "I would like to speak with you."

She cocks her head to one side, seemingly surprised, but answers, "Certainly, sir."

Durov's look of shock amuses me.

Although he may be the type of person to jump into a new experience, I need time to assess. I explain to them both, "I'd like to know a submissive's perspective in this power exchange."

Durov shakes his head in disappointment. "My gift wasted…"

Anderson winks at the sub. "If you're looking for something more, darlin', come see me afterwards. I'm a virgin, too."

She covers her smile and quickly looks down at her feet. I squeeze her hand as I guide her to a quiet area in a corner. I need to know if Durov's assertion, that this treatment is something she actively wants, is real.

"Absolutely," she assures me when I ask. "This is the only place where I am totally accepted for my kinky desires and needs."

I spend the next hour talking to her. I find it fascinating, the way her eyes light up when she talks about her various Doms. "Each one is so different." Her eyes drift to Durov. "But, I must admit, Rytsar is my favorite."

"Why is that?" I ask, wanting to know what his secret is.

She shakes her head, smiling at me. "He gets me. That man knows how to soothe my spirit even as he makes me cry out in severe pain." She lowers her eyes. "Can I tell you a secret?"

"Please do."

"I've never come as hard or as often as I do with Rytsar." She raises her eyes to meet my gaze. "He's able to mix my fear with sexual desire, and the results are the best orgasms of my life."

I glance at Durov with newfound respect. There is no doubt in my mind that she enjoys what he does to her.

"Being new at this, how does a Dom know what his submissive wants—or, more importantly, what she doesn't want?"

Her eyes sparkle when she tells me, "Communication. Sometimes we talk before a scene, especially if we are new to each other. Other times, I rely on my safeword."

"Durov talked about that. What is it, exactly?"

"It's the word my Master and I have agreed on to stop a scene. That way no one gets harmed." She grins. "Make no mistake, all of us subs at this dungeon are masochists, so we are hoping for pain. However, we trust our Masters will never harm us."

"And the difference between harming and hurting you?"

"Harming someone goes beyond the set limits and can result in permanent emotional or physical scars. That is not allowed here."

I look around the room at the women being whipped and tormented and see their experiences in a new light. "You can guarantee everyone here enjoys this?"

"Here? Yes. But there are places that do not adhere to safe practices. Those dungeons are dangerous for a girl like me. That's why I only play here."

"What makes them dangerous?"

"Not all dungeons vet their Doms. Nothing is more dangerous for a masochist than a wanna-be Dom. They seek only their own pleasure and do not care about us or the harm that they can cause."

"How were Anderson and I allowed in, then?"

"You being here means Rytsar has taken personal responsibility for your actions. He must really trust you both."

"I had no idea…" I say, glancing back at Durov.

"Rytsar is a good judge of character. Plus, I trust my own instincts and only get positive vibes coming from you and your friend."

I smile at her. "Most people find me too closed up

and serious."

"They must not be picking up on your natural dominance. It's understated, but very powerful, sir."

I can't help chuckling, thinking she is trying to flatter me. "You think so?"

"I do. Just like some Doms can tell when they run across a submissive, I can sense a Dominant a mile away." She blushes and adds, "Well, that's a bit of an exaggeration. Maybe a half-mile."

I laugh out loud, which seems incongruous with all the screaming and moaning going on around me.

According to her, some of her most memorable experiences have been with Dominants she's not collared to—including Rytsar Durov.

The idea of that type of relationship is a new concept to me, but it gives me hope. After the death of my father and the horrific scandal that followed, I swore off committed relationships and have satisfied my sexual desire by seeking random encounters to avoid entangling myself in something I cannot emotionally commit to.

But this...this is a profound exchange between a Dominant and submissive, built on a foundation of respect and trust. Emotional commitment is not a required element in the exchange.

Better yet, I would have control over their pleasure, which I plan to explore extensively.

"Do you mind if I touch your marks?" I ask her.

"Please, Master."

I balk at being called Master and tell her, "I'd prefer it if you simply call me sir."

She blushes. "Yes, Sir."

"What's your name?"

"I am called glee."

I smile, liking the name. It suits her well.

Reaching out, I tentatively caress the angry red marks on her skin. "These wounds…how long do they last, glee?"

She shivers under my gentle caress, looking at me with affection. "It depends. Most only last a few days." She runs her finger over one. "But each is cherished by me."

"Why?" I ask, circling the outer edge of a raise portion on her skin.

She trembles, her attention now solely focused on my touch. "They are physical reminders of the connection I shared with my Dom. I suppose it's kind of like the hickeys you get as a teenager."

"Ah…" I lightly trail my finger up her back to her neck. Testing my power over her, I demand, "Kiss me, glee."

She turns her head and leans forward, pressing her soft lips against mine. I instinctively flick my tongue against those tempting lips and feel the blood rush to my groin when she parts them for me.

Exploring the contours of her mouth, I begin imagining the things I would like to do to her body. Breaking the kiss, I stare at her for a few moments before asking, "Have you ever had an encounter here with a Dom who didn't use a whip or some kind of instrument?"

She giggles. "No, Sir."

"Would you like to try?"

At first, she smiles with amusement, but I watch as

her eyes grow wider the moment she realizes that I'm serious. "With you, I might."

"We'll consider it a date, then."

"Not tonight?" she asks, sounding disappointed.

"No. As Rytsar Durov has so crassly indicated, I'm new at this dynamic and would like to do a little research before I scene with you."

She bows, saying, "I would be honored to be your first when you return, if Rytsar wishes it."

When I hear a couple seriously going at it, I scan the dungeon. I'm surprised to see it's my roommate. Anderson appears to have found a woman who can take that massive shaft because he's balls deep in the woman, pounding away.

I'm happy for the guy. It's only taken him the entire fall semester to find her.

I notice Durov standing back, watching them. I have a sneaking suspicion he is the matchmaker, based on the pleased expression on his face.

My eyes drift back over to glee. "So, Rytsar isn't your Master?"

She giggles. "No." Glee points to another man who is using a cane to pleasure an older woman. "That's my Master. He has given Rytsar free reign over me."

I frown. "But won't your Master mind if I scene with you, instead?"

"Not if Rytsar has ordered me to."

I shake my head in disbelief. "There's a hell of a lot for me to learn."

Durov walks over and slaps me hard on the back. "*Da*, you have much to learn, but it's time we leave."

I take glee's hand and kiss it. "Until my return…"

She giggles again, blushing profusely.

Durov *tsks* in mock disgust. "There is no need for such niceties, comrade. You are missing the whole point if you think you must abide by vanilla rules."

"I disagree," I answer as I watch glee return to her Master. "I believe a woman deserves to be worshipped—especially when I plan to use her body solely for my pleasure."

# Anticipation

Anderson can't stop grinning as we make our way out of the warehouse.

Once outside, Durov abruptly stops us and warns, "You are not allowed to speak of this place or what happens here to *anyone*. I'm sure you can now appreciate the dynamic, and understand why it must remain a secret."

"I could certainly see jail time happening if we weren't careful," I agree.

"*Da*, there are many who do not understand what BDSM is and what it is not."

"Well, I have to admit I had no idea until tonight," Anderson states, his grin growing bigger. "If I had, I wouldn't have wasted the entire semester looking for what I found right here."

"Your cock will prove a real asset," Rytsar states.

Anderson sweeps back his hair. "Unbelievable. After all these years of having my cock sucked because I was too big to fuck a girl, I cannot express how incredibly satisfied I am right now."

"You do look like a man who's just had a good lay," I say with amusement.

"Good? It was fantastic! She took it all, and begged me to fuck her harder. I have *never* had a woman do that before."

Rytsar states proudly, "You will be very popular—and you are welcome."

Anderson holds out his hand to Durov. "I don't know how I can ever repay you, man."

"I'm sure I can find a way," the Russian replies, grinning mischievously.

We come across a payphone as we're walking back to the campus, and Anderson asks us to stop for a minute. "There's something I need to do."

He throws a bunch of change into the phone, and dials.

After a few seconds, we hear, "Hey, Ma? I know it's late, but do you mind shipping me the old bullwhip? I think it's still hanging in the barn." He pauses for a moment. "Yeah, yeah, that's the one. If you could send it Priority Mail, that would be great." After another extended pause, he asks, "Why do I need it?"

Looking over at us, he smiles. "Well…Ma, it's like this. I've been stressing over finals and thought a little bullwhip practice might take my mind off things."

He nods listening to her while gesturing for us to be patient.

"Sure, a batch of peanut butter cookies would be perfect." Anderson glances at me and says, "I'm sure he wouldn't mind." He cups the phone and asks, "My mom wants to send you cookies, too, and is wondering what kind you like."

I work hard to hide the foolish smile that threatens to spread across my face. I'm deeply touched that his mother thought of me. "I have no idea, to be honest."

Anderson whispers, "She makes killer Toll House cookies, man."

"Fine. Toll House it is."

Anderson speaks into the phone again. "Chocolate chip would be great, Ma. But I need you to get the package out tomorrow, if you can. I'm dying over here."

After he hangs up, Durov elbows me. "You're sharing those cookies with me, comrade."

I laugh. "That's a small price to pay for such an enlightening evening."

As we continue to walk, I grow silent, thinking back over the events of the night.

"Are you glad you came?" Durov asks, adding with an impish grin, "Despite the torture you were a witness to?"

I stop and put my hand on his shoulder, answering truthfully, "It's been a rare gift—this night."

"Do not squander it," he states before walking away.

I am filled with a sense of hope I haven't felt before. The idea that I might be able to overcome the scars I carry inside.

*To lead the semblance of a normal life—that would be a miracle.*

I look at Anderson and smirk. "I never would have guessed waking up this morning that this is how the night would end."

"Me either, buddy. This has been one fucking *crazy* night."

Looking at my watch, I smile at him. "And, it looks like I can still get in a few hours of study."

I fully expect him to give me shit about it, but I'm surprised when he opens the door to the building, stating, "Yeah, I think I'll join you tonight…"

Once finals are over, everyone starts heading home to spend Winter Break with their families, including Anderson.

I stay behind, wanting to be alone for the holidays, but Durov insists I stay with him at a beach house he's rented over the long break. It turns out his family has money—and lots of it.

"Are you sure? I don't have money to chip in for rent. Someday I will have more money than I need but, right now, I'm flat broke."

"Not a problem, comrade. Money is the least of my worries."

"Interesting, since money is the sole reason I'm here. I need to earn enough so I will never be vulnerable to anyone ever again."

"I understand that sentiment, but money doesn't solve everything." By the tortured look in his eyes, I know he is thinking of the person he lost.

I hope that over this long break, Durov and I will have the opportunity to share that darker side of ourselves. I have yet to find anyone who understands my pain, but I'm certain Durov will.

"Just so we're on the same page, you're not expecting Christmas gifts from me?" I ask him.

"God no," he says in his thick Russian accent. "I have no heart to celebrate this year."

Yes…there's no doubt Durov is the perfect person to spend this unwanted holiday with. I have come to despise Christmas, seeing it as only a painful reminder of everything I once knew. If I never see another Christmas tree or hear another holiday song, I will consider myself lucky.

"So, comrade, now that finals are over are you ready to return to the dungeon?"

*Am I?*

In preparation, I have spent countless hours studying BDSM. My desire is to give glee an experience she won't forget.

"Yes, but I have to admit I already feel the nerves setting in."

Durov scoffs. "Why?"

"It's my first time playing the role of a Dominant."

"Stop right there," he states firmly. "You can't walk into a scene with that attitude and expect to earn her respect. You are not playing a role, you *are* a Dominant."

"But, I'm completely inexperienced…"

"Dominance comes from here," he tells me, pressing the palm if his hand against my chest.

"What was your first time like?" I ask.

Durov smiles, thinking back on it. "It was…extremely gratifying."

"And you were not nervous at all?"

"*Nyet*. I grew up watching my father dominate women, so I was not nervous my first time."

"Well, without having the benefit of your background, I'm unsure how my scene with glee will play out."

"Do you have a goal in mind?"

"I do."

"Do you have experience with the instrument you will use?"

"I do."

"And, you have a safeword prepared?"

"Yes."

"Then stop fretting, comrade! Glee has been instructed to top you, if necessary. A successful scene is guaranteed."

"Top me?"

"*Da*. To take charge of the scene if she needs to guide you through it."

"I don't want to be topped."

Durov chuckles. "Most Dominants don't. But she has been ordered to, if needed."

While I see the wisdom of his plan, I'm determined to make sure glee will not have to guide me. I want the interaction between us to be a true D/s dynamic.

"Shall I let her know to meet us there tonight?"

The thought of dominating her sends a shiver of excitement through me, overriding my uncertainty. "Yes."

Durov's snorts in satisfaction. "Good. Tonight, we shall see what you are made of, comrade."

"Don't worry about me. You concentrate on your

own submissive tonight," I tell him.

He laughs. "What? You don't want me standing on the sidelines, critiquing you?"

"Absolutely not."

"That's what happened to me my first time."

"Who critiqued you?" I ask, fascinated.

"My father."

"Holy shit, and you still claim you weren't nervous?"

"I knew I would be a better Dom than he was, so his opinion didn't matter."

I have to say Durov's level of confidence is something to admire. It doesn't seem to come out of a false sense of bravado, but from a sincere belief in himself.

I hope to harness that level of confidence while scening with glee tonight. My primary goal is to explore her body with complete freedom while leaving her quivering after multiple orgasms.

The thought of having free reign over her body already has my cock hard...

# Virgin Territory

I dress up for the evening. Although I noticed during my last visit to the dungeon that the majority of the Doms wear black leather, I decide to wear my best Italian suit.

I always dress up for important occasions.

"Is that really how you're going, comrade?" Durov asks with a bemused smirk.

"Indeed," I tell him, straightening my tie.

"But a suit is impractical when wielding a whip."

"I know."

Durov's lips curl into a smile. "Well, tonight should prove entertaining at least."

When we arrive, the men in the dungeon eye me in silence as Durov and I enter the room. I'm sure they're convinced I have no clue what I'm doing, but they would be wrong. I stride through the dungeon and up to my submissive with confidence.

The minute glee sees me, her mouth opens in surprise and her cheeks blush a pretty shade of pink.

"Sir…" she says in an awe-filled voice as she lowers herself to the floor in a bow.

*That* is the response I am looking for.

Now that I have her attention, I command, "Stand and serve me."

Glee keeps her gaze to the floor as she stands up. I understand that not making eye contact is considered a sign of respect for submissives here but, as her Dominant, my will takes precedence.

"Undress with your eyes on me."

Meeting my gaze, glee begins to strip. First exposing her small, pert breasts before revealing her smooth, shaved pussy. I slowly circle her, admiring her firm, round buttocks, and the butterfly tattoo on the small of her back.

She is a masochist by nature, so I understand what she is expecting from this session, but I plan to expand her horizons just as she is going to expand mine.

"Do you wish to be challenged?" I ask her.

Her face lights up. "Oh, yes. Please!"

Wanting to build her anticipation further, I add, "Tonight your safeword is mercy."

"Oh, that is a sexy word, Sir," she purrs.

It's my belief that the mind is as much a playground as the physical body. I not only want my touch to linger on her body, but I want it to remain in her mind long after the evening is over.

I look around the room and choose an unoccupied spanking bench. When I go to help her onto it, she naturally lays on her stomach so her ass is exposed.

I tell her, "I want you to lie on your back, and place

your feet on either side where your knees would normally rest."

She gives me a surprised look, but quickly changes position.

I hear some of the men snickering in the background, certain my inexperience is already getting the best of me.

The restraints attached to the bench are not made for this position, so I grab some rope off the extensive wall display. While binding her ankles to the leg rest, I ask her, "Do you want your arms bound to your sides or above your head?"

"Above my head, Sir."

"Good. I like the way the position emphasizes your breasts," I reply lustfully as I take her wrists and move them above her head before binding them together.

My hands slowly trail from her bound wrists, down her arms, to her chest. Pinching her erect nipples between my fingers, I am rewarded with her soft moans. I tug on them, but get little response, so I pinch them harder.

Glee cries out in pleasure to my much more aggressive caress.

Leaning in close, I ask as I pull on her nipples again, "So you like it when I do this?"

"Oh, yes…I do, Sir."

Grasping both breasts in my hands, I squeeze them hard before bending over to take a nipple in to my mouth. Sucking, I pull away with her nipple still clenched in my teeth. I hear her squeak as she writhes on the spanking bench. Finally, I release her nipple. She moans with pleasure, begging me to do it again.

This time, as I take her nipple into my mouth, I place my hand on her bare mound. Glee is wet, obviously enjoying our session so far.

Little does she know what's in store for her…

I take off my jacket and lay it on a table. I then begin rolling up my sleeves as I stare at her hungrily.

Glee meets my gaze, her eyes wide with anticipation as I slip my finger into her pussy. I feel for her G-spot and begin circling it with my middle finger to stimulate it.

Once it begins to swell, I change tactics. With one hand pressed against her pelvis, I begin thrusting my finger into her as if I am fucking her with my cock. I am very purposeful in my rhythm and timing.

She instinctively stiffens in response to having her G-spot rubbed repeatedly.

"Relax," I command, stopping momentarily as I bend down and suck on a nipple before continuing.

After several minutes of stimulation, I start thrusting harder, mindful of keeping my fingers in direct contact with her G-spot. She starts panting and moaning. Soon, I hear the juicy sounds of her thoroughly wet pussy, but I am just getting started.

I have been curious after my laundry room encounter, wondering if every woman can gush with a watery come.

To have glee offer me her body is not only a sexual turn on, but a mental one as well. Being able to explore her body without the normal barriers imposed on us by society is a freedom I never thought possible.

I look down at her, lying naked on the table, tied up

and completely at my mercy—my submissive. It is the trust I see in her eyes, despite her vulnerability, that inspires me and I will do everything in my power not to break it.

Around me, women are screaming, some even crying, as they receive the intense attention of their Doms. I sneak a quick glance in Durov's direction and see he has a woman bound to an unusual wooden cross, something I believe is called a St. Andrew's Cross. Instead of the multi-tailed whip he used last time, Durov is holding a wicked looking paddle with holes in it. The girl begs him, "Rytsar, please make it hurt."

"Oh, I will, slave," he laughs huskily.

Her cries of pain soon follow.

I return my attention to glee. Continuing with the manual stimulation, her thighs begin to tremble and she cries out in pleasure when I bring her to orgasm but, to my disappointment, she has not produced the come I was seeking from her.

After her pussy stops pulsing from the climax, I insert my fingers again. Remembering how hard I pounded the girl in the laundry room, I ramp up the tempo of my thrusting.

Glee tenses. After several minutes, she starts whimpering, "I don't know what's happening."

"Relax and give into it, glee," I order, feeling that I am close.

She looks at me and I feel her physically relax even as I begin thrusting my fingers into her rapidly. Glee's pussy becomes extremely juicy from my focused attention, and the wet sound of it fills my ears, letting me know I'm close.

Sweat rolls down my brow as glee begins screaming. The speed at which I am thrusting seems almost violent, but the lust I see in her eyes spurs me on to continue.

Just as I am about to stop out of sheer exhaustion, I feel her body tense all over.

"Oh, Sir…oh, Sir…" she cries out in surprise.

All of the sudden, I feel the warm gush of liquid as glee orgasms for me. It flows from her, covering my hand before falling to the floor with a splash.

"What was that?" she cries, looking up at me in astonishment.

"You just came for me."

"But I've never done it like that before," she says, panting heavily.

"Did you like it?" I ask, legitimately curious.

She nods, still panting. "It was incredibly intense. I'm shocked my body can even do that."

I bring my fingers up to my nose, taking in the sweet-smelling aroma. Encouraged, I lick my fingers and smile at her. "It tastes sweet."

"Does it?" she asks in surprise.

I insert my finger into her quivering pussy, covering my finger with her essence before bringing it to her mouth. "Taste."

Glee opens her lips and I inset my finger into her mouth. She begins to suck on it. The intimate sexual exchange has my cock aching with need.

Her eyes grow wide as she tastes her own come for the first time. "Wow…" she whispers.

"Would you like to try again?"

"Yes, Sir," she answers with excitement.

I reposition myself, playing with her clit to prepare her body again before penetrating her with my fingers. Knowing the amount of thrusting required, I do not start out slowly.

Soon, her screams fill the room as her back arches in response to her building orgasm. I am relentless as I bring her to another watery climax even more intense than the first.

As her cries quiet, I'm suddenly aware that the dungeon has become silent. I look up to see the other Doms staring at me. I ignore them, turning my focus back on glee, wanting to know how many more times I can make her come like this.

"Ready for more?"

"I am yours, Sir."

Her simple answer makes my cock grow harder. Leaning down, I suck on her breasts, biting them lightly before returning my attention back to her pussy. Having complete control over her is a heady power.

"You will come over and over again until I am satisfied."

"Yes, Sir…" she whispers breathlessly.

I play with her pussy to the music of her passionate screams, and I don't stop until her entire body is covered in sweat and her own juices, as her thighs quiver uncontrollably after the last orgasm ends.

I watch her chest rise and fall rapidly as she lays there, her eyes half-open and dazed, too exhausted to move.

For the first time, I feel like a Dominant.

I look over at Rytsar and smile at him with newfound

confidence.

He strides over, placing a hand on my shoulder as he glances at glee. "I didn't know she was a squirter."

"I didn't know, either," she murmurs.

The Russian looks at me proudly. "You are full of surprises, comrade."

I look down at glee and see she is still trembling. "I'm not finished with her yet."

"By all means, continue," Rytsar replies, standing back.

I undo glee's bindings, wiping away the aftermath of our encounter before I lift her up and carry her to a quiet corner of the dungeon.

Sitting down, I cradle her against my chest. "Thank you, glee."

She lifts her head to look at me. "No, thank you, Sir. You are perfect."

I chuckle, leaning down to kiss her lightly on the forehead. She moans softly in response, wrapping her arms around the back of my neck as she pulls herself up to kiss me.

My shaft hardens in response, pressing against her. She looks down with a smile and asks sweetly, "May I suck on your cock, Sir?"

I nod.

Noticing she is slow in her movements, drained by our encounter, I undo my belt and pants, freeing my cock as she settles between my legs.

Sighing in satisfaction, she wraps her lips around my aching cock and begins slowly bobbing up and down. I close my eyes, concentrating on the glorious sensation. Unlike times before when my cock was too sensitive to hold back, I find that my prolonged state of arousal has made it possible for me to control myself much longer than anticipated.

I open my eyes to watch her mouth slowly descend on my cock before pulling up as she sucks hard. The slow and constant stimulation is extremely pleasurable, but there comes a point when I need more.

I start thrusting into her mouth, and glee instinctually speeds up her rhythm. Groaning in pleasure, I growl huskily, "Good girl."

I let the ache build as my climax approaches. Glee grasps my shaft with one hand, adding to the sensation. Taking profound satisfaction in the success of the scene I've played out with glee, my climax consummates the power exchange between us.

It is by far the best orgasm I have ever experienced. I don't hold back as a low, guttural cry escapes my lips as I come.

I pet glee's hair afterward, grateful for her submission. That feeling of hope I felt the first night Durov introduced me to the dungeon has grown stronger after tonight.

The intimate connection I feel with glee now is a by-product of the power exchange we've just experienced. The possibility of relating to women on this profound level, without the entanglement of emotional ties, is life changing for me.

Hell, who knows? There may even come a time when I will be able to open myself up to love.

I smile down at glee, grateful to Durov for opening up a whole new world to me.

# His Truth

Durov is silent on the drive back to the beach rental. Once there, however, he immediately gets out two tumblers and a bottle of vodka.

"This is cause for celebration!" he states as he heads back into the kitchen and grabs a bottle of pickles from the refrigerator.

"You do know the legal age for drinking is twenty-one?"

"That law was made for irresponsible drinkers. Are you an irresponsible drinker, comrade?"

"No."

"Then the law does not apply to us."

"That's not how it works," I chuckle.

"*Da*, it is."

He pours a generous amount of vodka into each glass.

"How did you get this vodka, anyway?" I ask.

"I have Russian connections," he answers with a smirk, "and I drink only the best."

Handing a glass to me, he holds his up to make a toast. "To a magnificent first scene."

I nod to him in appreciation, holding up my glass before I knock back the strong liquor. It burns all the way down my throat. Following Durov's lead, I take one of the pickles and immediately consume it afterward.

He grins at me. "You were impressive, comrade."

"Thanks," I reply, humbled by his praise.

"To go from seeming like a joke when you walked in, to having a dungeon full of sadists captivated by your scene, is reason to celebrate more!" Durov exclaims as he pours us another round of vodka.

I down the next one and feel the heat of the alcohol seeping into my veins.

Durov grins at me with a proud look in his eye. "I'm glad to know you, comrade."

"Likewise," I answer, still riding the high left over from the scene. I wouldn't be here tonight if it hadn't been for Durov inviting me to his secret BDSM club.

I owe him.

When Durov starts to pour another shot, I have to laugh.

He looks at me seriously, handing me back my glass. "Vodka opens up the soul, and you and I have much to talk about tonight."

I realize he's preparing to talk about his loss. I'm uneasy about the pain this conversation will bring for both of us, so I quickly slam down the shot of vodka.

"Do not forget the pickle, comrade. It helps lessen tomorrow's hangover."

"Really?" I dutifully pick up another small dill pickle

and take a bite.

"*Da*, we Russians are experts when it comes to consuming vodka," he says with a wicked grin.

Looking at Durov, I do not see a kid of eighteen. Although his face is young, his overall countenance is that of a man much older. The haunted look in his eyes reminds me of my own grief and, for a moment, I consider stopping the conversation before it starts—for both our sakes. But the desire to understand and to be understood overrides my mounting fear.

Durov sets down his glass, walks over to the sliding glass door facing the ocean, and opens it wide. Although the night is pitch black, the soothing sound of the waves enters the room, enveloping me.

With the warmth of the vodka flowing through my blood, I find the sound instantly calming.

The Russian turns back to me. "What we discuss tonight stays between us."

"Of course."

"No one, outside of those involved, knows what happened…" The graveness in his tone speaks to the profound level of sorrow he carries.

"I suspect we share a similar pain," I tell him.

"Do you feel responsible?" he asks, his eyes filling with tears.

"I do."

He nods his head.

Durov says nothing for a while, and I do not push him, knowing how hard it is to voice such things aloud.

"Have you ever been in love, comrade?"

I instantly think back to Isabella, my childhood

sweetheart. Her family was more than our good friends; they were as much a part of my family as my own blood relatives. Isabella had a kind heart, as well as being beautiful and exceedingly intelligent. At a young age, her talent as a musician was unquestionable and only served to cement my devotion to her.

We'd grown up together from the time we were infants and were the best of friends. I never questioned that I would marry her someday. Both families knew this and approved—but that all changed two years ago.

I am not that boy now.

I have no interest in marriage, and would only bring Isabella pain if we wed.

"No, I have never been in love," I tell him.

"Well, I have," he informs me. "I found my soul mate—and I will never love another."

"Those are strong words coming from someone who's only eighteen."

"It is the truth," he states in a sober tone. "Tatianna…" His voice breaks saying her name aloud. Durov closes his eyes, but the tears still fall. After several minutes, he clears his throat and looks at me. "I have not said her name since that day."

I only nod, knowing there are no words of comfort I can give.

"When I lost her, I didn't think I could survive. Even now…I struggle."

The hairs rise on the back of my neck. I understand exactly what he is saying.

"How long ago did you lose her?"

His face loses all color when he answers in a distant

voice, "I lost her just before spring."

"Six months ago?" I'm shocked by how recent his loss is.

"March 8." He chuckles sadly, adding under his breath, "On International Women's Day."

I am only vaguely familiar with the Russian holiday but, knowing that it centers on celebrating women, the fact that she died on that day must hold all kinds of complicated emotions for him.

When he looks up at me, I find myself suddenly overwhelmed—as if his pain is mine. "She died on March 8 by her own hands, but the truth is, my beautiful Tatianna died long before that."

"I'm sorry, Durov."

"My name is Anton."

I nod. "Anton."

He looks at me expectantly. After trusting me enough to share that part of his past, it's only natural he would expect me to return that trust—but I still hesitate to tell him my given name.

Durov, however, is a stubborn soul and lets the silence between us grow to an uncomfortable level.

Not wanting to lose our growing friendship, I throw caution to the wind, telling him my name even though I promised myself I never would. "You can call me Thane."

Durov stares at me in silence, but I can see the look of recognition slowly coming to his eyes. "*The* Thane Davis," he states.

"Yes."

He shakes his head. Instead of words of condemnation or even sympathy, he asks, "What really happened to your father?"

I'm left momentarily speechless. If he knows who I am, he knows all about the scandal surrounding my family. Surely, he must know what happened that day.

"My father took his own life."

"I know this, but why?" he presses.

Tears prick my eyes remembering the events that led up to that day. I boil it down to the simplest terms. "I kept a secret that killed him."

Durov's eyes narrow. I'm fully prepared to be questioned, but he tells me, "I thought it was true the moment I met you—we are meant to be brothers."

His reaction is the last thing I expected. His acceptance of me after revealing my darkest truth, bonds me to Durov in a way I never imagined.

"As for me, my beautiful Tatianna is dead because I failed to protect her. If I had it to do over again..." He pauses, then looks at me with those tortured blue eyes. "Well, it doesn't matter—does it?"

I shake my head in agreement. "No, we cannot change the past. It is the cruelest part of surviving the suicide of someone you love. You relive it every day, but you will never be able to alter the events that led to their death."

"*Nyet*. You are condemned forever for your failure."

I shudder, the truth of his words sending a cold chill through me.

"How did your father die?" Durov asks.

The blood and violence of that moment flashes through my mind, and I struggle to speak. "Gunshot."

He only nods.

"What about Tatianna?"

He chokes on the words as he speaks, "She…slit her wrists."

Knowing how recent her suicide was, I can only imagine what he is going through emotionally. At six months, I wasn't able to talk about it with anyone—not even the therapists.

"My father apologized to me before shooting himself in the head," I confess to Durov. "He died in my arms."

Tears form in Durov's eyes. "I do not think I could have borne such a thing."

"So you walked in after she had died?" I ask quietly.

The look he gives me is full of such raw pain, it steals my breath away.

"I came bearing flowers…" Durov starts sobbing uncontrollably and immediately turns away from me.

I walk over to him, his pain my pain. Pushing past the walls I have built up, I put my arms around him, giving him my strength. He resists only for a moment before burying his head in my chest and crying openly.

I hold back my own sorrow. The pain he is suffering is so new, he has no mechanisms to deal with it.

I've had two years.

I know how to compartmentalize that unbearable pain.

# Moy Droog

The two of us talk well into the night, and I open up to him like I have never done before with anyone.

"My father was incredibly talented. His music literally changed people's lives based on the numerous letters he received from around the globe. Everyone loved him, and yet...he still treated me like I was what mattered most to him."

"*Moy droog*, I am envious of the close relationship you had with your father, even though it ended tragically," Durov tells me. "My father has only earned my deepest resentment."

"Why?" Following his example, I pour a glass of vodka and hand it to him to help ease the conversation.

Taking it from me, Durov downs the liquor angrily before speaking. "I have four brothers. As a family we should be strong together, but my father destroyed that. In every way he could, he made me the outcast in my own family. I am utterly alone except for my mother."

He closes his eyes and murmurs under his breath,

"*Mamulya…*"

Hearing him speak of his mother sets me on edge. "Unlike you, I'm an only child, and you know the scandal the erupted in the media following my father's death. I never imagined I could feel so alone at the age of fifteen."

"I understand that feeling, *da,*" he says in solemn voice.

"As only someone unfortunate enough to walk in our shoes could," I mutter, downing my own drink.

"Agreed, *moy droog.*"

I know the Russian phrase means "my friend". After being isolated and alone for so long, he cannot know what those two simple words mean to me.

I pour another shot for both of us and hold my glass up to him. "*Moy droog.*"

He smiles before gulping down the vodka and grabbing another pickle. "So, what happened to your mother? The scandal was all over the news and then she virtually disappeared."

The question jars me even though I should have expected it. Just as I did with my roommate, I hide my instinctual reaction whenever my mother is mentioned, but I surprise myself by admitting something I have kept buried because I'm ashamed.

"Do you know I loved my mother deeply? Possibly even more than my father?"

Oh God, how it hurts, facing that truth now…

In the span of a few years I've lost everything—my parents, my innocence, and all I've held to be true. "I will tell you about her someday, Anton. However, I am unwilling to discuss what happened now."

*No amount of vodka could open up those floodgates.*

Durov nods in understanding. "You and I hold many secrets only we and God know."

"I would agree, except I don't believe in a God."

He stares at me in shock. "You don't?"

I shake my head. "How can I? No omniscient being who 'cares' would allow the things that have happened to us."

"I beg to differ, *moy droog*. God may be all-knowing, but he cannot interfere. To do so would be the same as treating us like caged animals. Manipulating our fates is no different than putting us in prison and robbing us of free will. Change only happens under adversity. Who would want to live in a world where everything was given to us without a struggle? We would be no different than pet rabbits."

"Well, I for one do not care to live in a world where violence and pain is the norm."

"But it's not, comrade," he insists. "Think of your friend Anderson. He has no idea what real pain is, having been spared of it growing up. It's not by design but by chance that we have faced the things we have. Life is a balance—for there to be good in the world, there must also be bad. Our time will come, eventually. I'm sure of it."

"If you believe it's all chance, than why believe there is a God?"

"Because there is an order and beauty to the world that cannot be explained," he states.

I have never admitted to anyone that there have been

times when I've been alone in the dark, trying to sleep, and have questioned why the natural world always seems to obey the laws of mathematics. As Durov said, there seems to be an order that makes no sense unless there is a Creator who set the mathematical foundation that makes of our universe fathomable.

"While I may agree with you on some level, Durov, the idea that an omniscient being would stand back and watch his creations suffer seems cruel and inhumane."

Durov laughs. "Not if he's a sadist."

"God as a sadist…now there's something I never considered," I chuckle.

His voice has almost a wistful tone to it when he tells me, "I've had moments when the simple beauty of a sunset, the immensity of the universe, or the sheer miracle of life itself has humbled me to the core. I do not question if there is a Creator because the proof of His work is all around me."

"If that is true, then I have a question for you."

"What?"

"How do we get in God's good graces?"

Durov throws back his head and laughs. "*Moy droog*, if I knew that, I would not be here with you now."

With uninterrupted time on our hands, I ask Durov if we can visit the dungeon so I can observe and learn. I'm like a sponge as I watch the other Dominants interacting with their submissives.

Durov has previously informed me that most of the Masters at this dungeon are sadists, and I can already tell that that is not where my interests lie.

I enjoy exploring a woman's body, finding out where her erogenous zones are so that I can tease and torment them with pleasure rather than pain. However, I am curious about the pain aspect of masochism, and I wonder if it can act as an aphrodisiac even for those who are not so inclined.

"*Moy droog*, I like your enthusiasm!" Durov tells me when I ask to go to the dungeon after having just visited it the night before.

"There is so much to learn. Although there are aspects of BDSM I can acquire from books, observation is proving far more valuable to me."

He smacks me on the back. "You have a lifetime of learning ahead, comrade. There is no need to learn it all at once. Although observation is valuable, it's important to dip your feet in."

I understand what he is saying but I am a perfectionist at heart, and I do not handle failure well in even the smallest of details. It's the reason I excel in whatever I put my mind to, but I realize it also holds me back.

It is one weakness of mine...

The smell of leather, sweat, and sex invades my nostrils as we enter the dungeon. Determined to push myself, I feel a heightened sense of exhilaration.

"What do you want to do, *moy droog*?"

"I would like to observe first."

He rolls his eyes, sounding disappointed. "Of course."

I don't mind Durov giving me a hard time, because I know his tune will change when I make my request later tonight.

I scan the room looking, for something new I haven't seen played out before. I find it in Mistress Azure. She has her submissive bound to a table, naked, her ankles tied to the legs of the table and her ass resting on the edge, the perfect level for fucking.

The submissive's wrists are bound at her sides, with her neck held in place with metal restraints bolted to the table and secured with locks. The woman is completely helpless, and knowing that turns me on.

The Mistress prepares, meticulously placing each item she is going to use on a tray—antiseptic liquid, cotton balls, a set of nipple clamps, gloves and two long needles. She looks as her submissive when she is done and smiles.

"Are you excited, songbird?"

The girl can only stare up at the ceiling because the neck restraint holds her in place, but she replies excitedly, "I am, Mistress."

"You have waited a long time for this."

The girl grins when she answers, "I have."

Mistress Azure wets a cotton ball with the antiseptic, then, with the sensual movements of a lover, she coats the sub's left nipple. The coldness of the liquid drying on her skin causes both the sub's nipples to harden into peaks.

I notice the girl's chest rising and falling more rapidly as her mistress sets the used cotton ball down. Mistress Azure begins speaking to the girl in low tones that only she can hear while caressing her lower stomach in concentric circles with her long fingernails.

The act itself is very erotic, and I watch with growing interest.

The Domme leans down and hesitates for a moment before lightly kissing the top of her submissive's bare mound.

The girl whimpers in pleasure.

Her Mistress picks up one of the nipple clamps and places it on the areola of her left breast, tightening it so the nipple stands pert and ready for attention. She then lightly stimulates it with her fingers, causing the girl to moan with pleasure.

Mistress Azure picks up the gloves and slowly slips them both onto her hands, purposely standing where her sub can see her. She never takes her eyes off the girl, drawing out every second, intentionally building up the tension.

I admire how she keeps her sub her sole focus the entire time. Even though they are playing this scene out in public, the intimate way she treats her submissive makes it feel as if they are alone in a private setting.

I prefer that to the grandstanding some of the Dominants indulge in when they scene at the dungeon with a sub. It's obvious to me that, based on those Doms' words and actions, they are catering to their own egos.

I find it tiresome.

Fortunately, Mistress Azure is gracing me with a peek into what it must look like when a D/s scene is played out in the privacy of the bedroom.

She picks up one of the needles and runs her fingers

down the length of it. "Are you ready, songbird?"

Her sub answers enthusiastically, "Yes, Mistress."

I unknowingly hold my breath as I watch the Domme grip the nipple clamp with one hand as she sets the sharp needle against the girl's tender flesh.

Again, she hesitates for a moment, drawing out this experience, before slowly inserting the large needle through her nipple.

The girl gasps and then starts moaning in pain as the needle pieces the skin. Her Mistress praises her as she continues to push it slowly through the nipple and out the other side.

"Oh, yes," Mistress Azure purrs. "You did well, songbird."

The girl is breathing quickly, her body covered in goosebumps.

"And now for the second one."

Having just experienced it, the girl is familiar with the level of pain involved. I know she has been given a safeword but, instead of calling it, she says, "Thank you, Mistress."

Her Domme moves even slower as she prepares the second nipple, and it is easy to see the girl is completely focused on her Mistress's every touch and movement.

After she places the second needle against her nipple, she asks, "What do you want, songbird?"

"I want to feel the needle, Mistress."

"Your wish is my command," Mistress Azure murmurs, as she slowly pushes the needle through her right nipple. Again, the girl cries out, her breath coming in short gasps.

"I want you to relish this pain. This is all for you."

Once the needle is in place, Mistress Azure takes off her gloves and leans over her sub. "Brace yourself, pet."

The Domme takes hold of both nipple clamps and releases them at the same time.

The girl stiffens as the blood rushes to her nipples and her moans can be heard throughout the dungeon.

Once she quiets, her Mistress purrs, "I am not done with you yet."

Mistress Azure moves where her submissive can see her, commanding her to watch as she straps on a black dildo with the same sexual titillation she would be using if she were doing a striptease.

She then covers the thick phallus with lubricant, moaning seductively as she grasps it and rubs the whole length repeatedly with her hand.

After cleaning off, Mistress Azure leans down and kisses her sub on the lips. "I am going to fuck you until you scream."

Songbird makes little excited chirping sounds as her Mistress moves into position. I now understand the reason for her pet name.

Knowing the girl cannot see what her Mistress is doing because of the metal restraint around her neck adds to the excitement of the scene. I like the element of the unknown that the restraint adds and must applaud Mistress Azure.

Mistress Azure's eyes shine with lust as she begins by rubbing the dildo against her sub's pussy, coating it with lubricant from the dildo before thrusting it into her.

Songbird becomes completely silent while her body

is forced to take the length of the shaft. Mistress Azure then grabs her hips and begins fucking her with the phallus. Her strokes are slow but deep, challenging the sub with each thrust.

When the Domme begins rolling her hips in a circular motion, I notice the goosebumps returning to the girl's skin and the chirping starts up again.

"Tell me when you're close," Mistress Azure commands as she leans forward, forcing the dildo even deeper.

Soon the girl starts panting. "Oh...oh...ohhh...."

My cock hardens the closer she gets to climaxing, and it almost feels as if I am joining in their sexual experience.

"Mistress...!" she finally cries.

The Domme thrusts hard, then leans in. "Yes, songbird?"

"I'm close, so close..."

"Good girl."

Mistress Azure leans in, giving a powerful thrust while reaching up and flicking the needles piercing her nipples.

The girl's mouth falls open as her back arches and her eyes roll back, no sound escaping her lips. Then her whole body starts shaking violently as an intense orgasm overtakes her.

Mistress Azure holds herself still, but continues to flick the needles as her sub orgasms. A loud scream escapes her sub's lips just before her whole body stiffens and becomes still.

Pulling out, the Domme pets her sub's swollen pussy. She unstraps the dildo and lays it gently on the table.

Walking up beside her sub's head, she moves a strand of hair from her face. "Nothing is more satisfying that a long-awaited reward..." she murmurs as she unlocks the neck restraint and undoes all the bindings.

The sub has yet to move or respond to her. Mistress Azure begins caressing her face. "Return to your Mistress."

When the girl remains unresponsive, the Domme slaps her face lightly. "Songbird."

I see the girl's eyes flutter momentarily, and then she opens them wide and looks up at her Mistress, smiling.

"I screamed, Mistress."

"Yes, you did," she purrs, leaning down to kiss her.

With the scene complete, I turn away, commanding my cock to calm the fuck down as I leave in search of the Russian.

# Learning by Example

I walk up just as Durov is finishing his own scene. The older sub he was just playing with is still crying, her back covered in large welts.

Durov lifts her chin up and kisses her hard, obviously turned on by the intense power exchange. "Your tears bring me great pleasure," he tells her.

Her gaze slowly turns from him to the whip in his hands. "Your cat-o'-nines frees me like nothing else can."

Durov unbinds her and orders, "Kiss it."

With reverence, she takes the wicked looking leather strands that have caused the many angry looking marks on her back and kisses each one. Afterward, she smiles up at him gratefully.

"Thank you, Rytsar."

He nods with satisfaction. "You may go."

She seems a little unsure on her feet when she gets up, so Durov holds out his hand and helps her to balance.

"Thank you again, Rytsar," she replies with a respectful bow before she leaves.

Durov pounds his chest afterward. "How I love playing with my 'nines!"

"It must have been intense, based on the numerous welts on her back and that huge grin on your face," I tell him.

He grins even wider as he looks in her direction. "It was, comrade! She had much to release."

While he begins the task of cleaning off his whip, I decide the time has come to make my request. "Durov."

"Yes, *moy droog?*"

"I want to understand how pain can translate into pleasure and would like you to teach me."

He smirks. "Why not learn from the best?"

I chuckle, amused by his cocky self-assurance. However, based on how the submissives in the dungeon flock to him, I know his confidence is not misplaced.

I start unbuttoning my shirt.

Durov stares at me with a look of shock. "What are you doing?"

"I want you to teach me using your cat-o'-nines," I answer, glancing at the harsh instrument he holds in his hand as I shrug off my shirt.

He looks at me in stunned silence when I lay my shirt on a chair and walk over to a pole, putting my wrists in the metal bindings.

"*Nyet.*"

I turn my head back toward Durov, concerned that I've offended him. "What do you mean *no?*"

"I will not do it like this," he growls, spitting on the

ground. "It…reminds me too much of my childhood."

I'm unsure what has him upset, but I bring my arms down slowly and turn to face him. "How can I understand it if I don't experience it myself?"

"True, comrade…" His shakes his head, chuckling when he adds, "But when I suggested you to dip your feet in, I never thought this is the direction you would go."

I'm not embarrassed by my request and ask, "How can I be an effective Dominant if I don't experience the receiving end? It's the only way to truly understand the connection between pain and pleasure that so many submissives here seem to thrive on."

He frowns. "Do you consider yourself a masochist by nature?"

"No. Pain is definitely not the way I derive sexual pleasure."

"Then that makes what you are proposing even more difficult."

"Too much of a challenge for you, Durov?"

He snorts. "I like your tenacity, comrade." Glancing around the room, he mutters quietly to me, "However, we may never hear the end of it in this dungeon if I go through with the scene."

"If it happens, so be it," I reply. "I've been dragged through the coals in front of the whole world, so ribbing by a handful of Doms will be a cakewalk for me."

Durov raises an eyebrow. "You know, you would not be the only virgin here."

"What do you mean?" I ask, thinking he's kidding.

"I have never scened with a man before."

I chuckle. "Great. Two virgins doing it for the first time in front of an audience of sadists."

Durov laughs.

This is too important to me to joke about, so I look him in the eye and ask, "Are you willing to teach me?"

He sighs. "If I do this, I will have to make certain…adjustments."

"I trust you completely."

Durov smirks. "Maybe you shouldn't, *moy droog*."

Scanning the area, his eyes settle on a spot on the other end of the room. "There is where we'll do it," he tells me, pointing. "Get my submissive shade," he barks to one of the subs standing nearby. "Tell her I need her *now*."

The girl bows and runs off.

"Let me think on this," Durov says as he walks over to the area he's indicated. I watch as he stands back, his arms crossed. "The challenge of introducing someone inexperienced to painful stimulation is that I must balance it with pleasure for you to respond positively. Normally, I use my wand…" He frowns, as he stares hard at two thin metal pipes that run from the floor to the ceiling.

I have no idea what he is thinking, but remain respectfully silent while he contemplates how the scene should play out.

When shade arrives, breathless from running, she falls at his feet in a bow. "How may I serve you, Rytsar?"

Durov looks down at her and smiles. "How would you like to introduce a new Dom to the power of pain?"

She looks up briefly, her eyes shining with delight.

"It would be an honor, Rytsar."

Durov unfolds his arms and places his hand on her head. "Good."

Turning to me, he says, "I refuse to bind you. If you agree to do this, you will hold still by your own willpower."

"Fair enough." I am grateful he has agreed to teach me.

"Strip."

I stare at him. "Why? I'm only offering you my back, nothing else."

Durov raises an eyebrow, challenging me.

For the first time, I realize he may not have been kidding me about trusting him. Based on the wild glint in his eye, this might very well be a mistake. Still, the need to understand overrides my reservations.

I undress completely, standing in front of him without shame. "Now what?"

"You will grab onto the two pipes. There is no need for a safeword. If you don't want to continue, let go of the pipes and the pain will cease. It's as simple as that, *moy droog*."

Durov then looks down at shade. "Move to a safe distance and await my command."

Shade bows to him before repositioning herself.

He holds out the instrument to me. "Do you see there are nine tails and each one has a knot on the end?"

"Yes. I have studied the instrument before."

"Studied...ha!" His face breaks into a grin. "Touch each knot, comrade. Acquaint yourself with them, because soon you will feel the power and fierceness of these 'nines."

A chill runs through me as I finger the hard leather knots. I honestly have no idea what kind of pain I am about to experience, but there is something strangely intoxicating about the unknown.

"Grab the pipes and prepare yourself," he orders in a commanding voice.

The man I know has transformed before me. He is all Dom, and I have just given him free reign to school me. I spread out my arms and take a pipe in each hand. I look up at the ceiling, hoping I don't make a fool of myself once his lesson begins.

"Look straight ahead," he commands.

I do as he says, staring at the rough brick wall.

"I will leave marks," he informs me.

"Fine, but don't make them permanent."

He laughs in answer as he begins swinging his 'nines in order to warm up. I hear the tails cutting through the air and have only one thought:

*I hope to fuck I don't regret this…*

"No matter how painful it gets, comrade, you must remember to breathe."

"Heard."

"Let the lesson begin."

I close my eyes, waiting for that first strike, my mouth dry with anticipation.

Knowing it is coming, I'm still not ready for it when the 'nines make contact with my back. I hear the thud explode in my ears at the same time the knots strike my skin, but those fuckers don't just sting—they feel like they're literally cutting me.

I let out a low grunt, holding back the urge to cry out. By the second strike, I am able to keep silent, but I forget to breathe.

"Let it out," Durov commands.

I open my mouth to let out the breath I've unknowingly held inside, only to feel an even more intense volley of lashes. Once again, the only way to remain silent is to hold my breath.

"You *must* breathe through the pain," he orders.

I close my eyes, taking a moment to calm my racing heart and attempt to ignore the fiery pain engulfing my back while I mentally readjust my thoughts. I am obviously fighting against this experience when I have asked for it.

I begin taking slow, steady breaths, determined to stay focused no matter how much the whip shocks my system.

Taking in one long breath, I let it out slowly in preparation.

"Ready?"

"*Da*," I answer.

He chuckles under his breath, but with his amusement comes another volley of lashes even more severe than the last. Each one tests me, forcing the air out of my lungs as it strikes my back, but I dutifully take in another breath, only to have it knocked out again.

Durov stops and praises me. "Excellent. Now that you can breathe again, I will show you what real pain feels like."

My heart starts beating rapidly. I have only to let go of the pipes and all of this ends, but I am too invested to give up now.

I hear Durov bark, "Shade, go suck him."

I struggle to stay standing, my muscles trembling from the onslaught. My brain is not quite registering what is happening when shade gets down on her knees.

She takes my shaft in her hands and it instantly rises to attention.

With slow precision, she starts sucking, then pulls back before taking my cock in her warm mouth again. The girl is an expert with those lips, and although I can't ignore the fire that's overtaken my back, her mouth begins to soothe me.

I watch with rapt attention as those lips travel up and down my cock and her tongue curls around the head of it.

Without warning, Durov strikes me again with the 'nines and the unbearable fire returns while her mouth continues to arouse me.

"Deep throat him," he commands.

I moan in pleasure as she begins taking my rigid shaft deeper.

Again, the 'nines strike my back, momentarily obliterating all thought, but her mouth becomes my focus as she takes me down her throat even deeper.

"Are you watching her, comrade?"

"Yes," I answer, my voice hoarse with pain—and lust.

"Does she please you?"

"Very much," I groan as I watch her lips brushing against my dark pubic hair, my entire cock now encased in her tight throat.

I stop breathing when Durov begins unleashing his whip on my back without mercy. Lash after lash takes all reason away...

When he stops, I am literally shaking—my grip on the pipes the only thing keeping me standing.

The pain from the cat-o'-nines is all consuming. There is no other reality for me.

"Shade, continue," I hear him call as if from a great distance.

When she responds to him, her voice seeming equally far away.

I cannot process his words and struggle when I realize he is talking to me. Finally, he puts his hand on the back of my neck and squeezes hard, leaning in close.

"Face forward, *moy droog*. And do not move..."

My nerves kick into overdrive, having just experienced the ferocity of his cat-o'-nines, but there is a thrill associated with that fear.

I have no doubt Durov is about to transform my excruciating pain into pleasure.

Closing my eyes, I wait, concentrating on every sensation—from shade's incredible oral skills to the sound of Durov's heavy breathing.

"Hold very still," he reminds me.

I grip the pipes harder, bracing myself.

Shade takes my shaft in her hand, and I feel the alluring warmth of her lips. She encases my cock with her sexy mouth and teases me with that talented tongue before she begins sucking, drawing me down her tight throat again.

An expert at what she does, my heart begins racing

wildly as my climax builds. I groan lustfully while teetering on the edge of climax.

A bolt of burning lightning explodes across my back when the knotted tails hit, and it sends me over the edge. My whole body stiffens just before I orgasm.

I can't breathe…

The intensity of my climax is unlike anything I've experienced before, and I thrust my cock down her throat repeatedly.

The orgasm seems to go on forever, leaving me so drained afterward that I'm too weak to stand and slowly slide down the pipes until I'm kneeling on the floor. I wrap my arms around shade for support and hold her tight against me.

My muscles tremble violently, so I force myself to take in slow, measured breaths in order to regain control.

Durov's strong hand grasps the back of my neck and I feel his strength flow into me. "Do you understand now, *moy droog?*"

# Friends

It turns out that the month off from school hanging with Durov on the beach is cathartic for both of us. Although we cannot change what has happened in our pasts, we now have each other to lean on.

Life will never be the same for me...

When Anderson returns to campus, he not only looks refreshed but invigorated. "Oh hell, I wish you'd been there! Maybe next year you can join me in Colorado. You know my mama cooks the best down-home meals, and my sisters are a hoot."

"I bet they are."

He pulls a photo from his wallet, smiling broadly. "Here's our latest Christmas photo."

The picture makes me chuckle. The entire family is dressed in red sweaters, from him, his three sisters and his parents, to the damn dogs.

I note that his sisters all range in age, but they look similar to Anderson because of their intense green eyes and charming smiles. Knowing what a jokester he is, I can't imagine what it's like when all four siblings get together.

He points to his dad. "I know he looks all serious in this photo, but my dad…he's the biggest prankster of all. This Christmas he really outdid himself. You wouldn't believe what he pulled off."

Looking at Anderson, I can see in his face and in the lightness in his countenance that spending time with his family has revitalized him.

I want that.

"So, how did you spend Christmas?" he asks.

"Skipped the holidays altogether and concentrated on learning more about BDSM."

"How many hours did you spend at the library?" he teases.

"None."

His jaw drops.

"Did you go to the dungeon?"

I nod.

"Oh, now you've got me all jealous. How was it?"

Smirking, I tell him, "I'm light years ahead of you now. While you were making merry, I was learning how to be the better Dominant."

"Hah. I practiced my bullwhip every day while I was in Colorado. My mama even complimented my skills."

"Little does she know what you're planning to do with that whip," I laugh.

He grins, and I am shocked to see a blush coloring his cheeks. "Yeah, well… there *is* that."

"Want to head to the dungeon at the end of the week?"

Anderson stares at me and shakes his head several times. "Wait. You want to go out this weekend?"

Shrugging, I tell him. "There's more to life than studying."

"Did you get taken over by aliens over Christmas break? This is *not* the Davis I know and tolerate."

I smile. I have to admit that Anderson makes me laugh, and I've missed his humor this past month.

Looking at the glint in his eye, I can see he thinks he's already won our bet. That couldn't be further from the truth, but I'm happy to make him feel comfortable in that assumption.

"Can I bother you for some help?" he asks.

I naturally assume he is talking about needing prep work for a class he'll be starting this semester. Instead, he says, "While I may have practiced my bullwhip over winter break, there was one thing I couldn't do."

"What's that?"

"I couldn't practice my lighter touch on an actual human. I started with sacks of grain until I had perfected my stroke and then tried it on my favorite cow Betsy. She seemed fine with it—didn't even twitch an ear—but I'd like to know what it feels like so I can adjust if needed."

I frown. "Exactly what are you asking me?"

"Would you mind being my guinea pig?"

"Sorry, I'm still recovering from my session with Durov." I pull off my t-shirt and turn to show him my back, the few remaining marks still visible but healing.

*Fucking sadist.*

Anderson's jaw drops. "You and the Russian?"

I shrug. "I needed to know from experience how the whole pain and pleasure thing works."

He runs his hand through his hair while shaking his head. "I never would have thought…"

"You can stop right now. It was purely for learning purposes. No different than your request."

"So, what was your conclusion after your session with Durov?"

"I definitely experienced a stronger orgasm with the endorphins flowing, but I wonder if pain is the only way to achieve that level of climax. It has me curious, so I plan to explore it further using various methods."

"Interesting. You'll have to let me know how that goes for you." Staring at my back, he says, "You know, it wouldn't hurt. At least, if I get it right."

I snort. "What can't you ask a submissive? I'm sure there are plenty who would be willing."

"I don't want to fail my first time with a sub. You know? It would get in my head and fuck things up."

I nod, remembering how I'd felt the same way with glee. "Fine, I will sacrifice this one time, but I don't want this to become a *thing* between us."

He laughs. "No worries, buddy. You are not my dream date, no matter how much you try to convince yourself you are."

I frown. "You do realize you're asking me for a favor. It's not smart to insult the person you need help from."

"Sure thing, *Dad*."

"There you go again," I say, putting my shirt back on.

Anderson starts chuckling. "See, I've missed this. You and your old man wisdom."

I just nod slowly. "You think third time's a charm, do you?"

Anderson slaps me on the back. "Ah, you know you love it."

I cringe, my back still painfully sensitive.

As soon as he sees my expression, he sputters, "Oh, fuck...sorry, man. Totally forgot."

I know I have him eating out of my hand now. Glaring at him, I say, "I'm done here."

"No! I seriously didn't mean to hurt you, buddy."

"You repeatedly insult me, *then* you hit me when I've just showed you I was still healing."

"Dude, you've got to believe me!"

"Go find some other sap to tickle with your whip," I growl, starting toward the door.

"What do I have to do to convince you?" he cries.

I stop, turning around slowly. "It's simple. You will owe me, if I do this. And I'll have the right to call in that debt—anytime, anyplace."

"Really? I'm just supposed to give you a free pass for one tiny favor?"

"Yes," I tell him without cracking a smile. "Or you could ask Durov."

"Hell no, man. I don't trust that sadistic bastard."

I hold out my hand to him. "Deal?"

He stares at it for several seconds before taking it. "Deal."

"Fine. Find a secluded area sometime during the week, and show me how you tickled that cow over break."

I'm surprised when Samantha enters my Advanced Economics class at the start of the new semester. When she sees me, her face momentarily lights up, and then she remembers herself.

Straightening her back, she lifts her chin and walks toward me like a woman in charge. The thought runs through my head that she looks like a Domme, but I immediately laugh it away.

When she sits down next to me, I mutter to her, "If I didn't know better, I'd swear you were stalking me."

"Don't flatter yourself," she replies coldly, but I see the pink hue in her cheeks. She doesn't fool me with that icy response.

It's actually good to see her again, and I lean in to ask, "What's your semester look like?"

Her eyes soften, the cold persona dissolving as quickly as she created it. "All business classes this time, except for…" She looks at me, seemingly embarrassed to say.

"Go on, no judgments here," I assure her, knowing what I've been doing over the break.

"I'm taking a film class."

"Oh, more photography?"

She shakes her head slightly. "No. Professor Brooks suggested I take an introductory class in filmmaking."

"Really?" I knew the professor was highly impressed

with Samantha's photography skills, but I never would have guessed she'd suggest movies.

"Yeah, I know it seems foolish to waste my time, but…"

"Not at all. I think you should always pursue your talents."

"Even if they have nothing to do with your major?"

Before my introduction to BDSM, I would have thought otherwise, but now I understand the importance of opening oneself to new experiences.

"I respect Professor Brooks. I not only learned about the art behind shooting photos, but I also learned about myself in the process. If she recommends you should pursue film, I would seriously consider it. Although, I'm curious why she would suggest it, instead of taking a more advanced photography class."

Samantha's blush grows deeper when she tells me, "She said my creative eye and unique perspective would work best in film. I'm not sure if that was a compliment."

"It was definitely a compliment," I assure her. "Professor Brooks is not one to flatter or mislead."

"True."

I sit back and look at her. "So, am I looking at the next Spielberg?"

"No," she says with a half-smile. "I'll never get rich pursuing film. Who you are looking at is a future CEO of a top Fortune 500 company."

I nod my approval. "I'm sure I am."

For a moment, tears start to well up in her eyes, and I suspect she's thinking of something her brother once said. But, with a quick blink, they disappear.

Samantha's control over her emotions has improved considerably. I no longer feel uncomfortable around her. Her dogged determination to treat me as a friend rather than her brother's ghost has cemented our friendship.

After class, I ask her to join me for lunch. I notice that she still walks with her hands clutched around her books, which contrasts sharply with the women who walked into class just an hour ago.

I wonder about this change in her.

"How was your break?" I ask.

She glances at me sideways, frowning slightly, and says nothing. Apparently, that subject is off limits.

"What about you?" she finally asks.

Normally, I would have reacted just as she had. However, things have changed for me. Hell, I've changed. "Couldn't be better. Spent the entire time on the beach with one of my friends."

"A girlfriend?" she ventures.

"No, a Russian kid I met in my Molecular Biology class. You'd like him."

"Can't say I've ever met a Russian before."

"He's entertaining and boisterous—to say the least."

"Well, if he's a friend of yours, I'd like to meet him."

Out of the blue, I'm hit with an image of Samantha bound and gagged, with Durov standing behind her, his 'nines clutched in his hand. I shake my head, smiling to myself.

"What's so funny?"

"Nothing. Just a random thought," I tell her. I look at Samantha again, but I can't see her submitting to anyone. Instead, it's entirely possible she might enjoy the power of being a Domme.

It might even help break her from her past, the way it is helping me.

I decide to talk to Durov before I bring it up with her. It could be that a visit to his dungeon is exactly what Samantha needs. She just doesn't know it yet.

My conversation with Durov does not go the way I envisioned.

"Absolutely not!" he growls under his breath.

"Is it because she's a woman?" I ask, insulted that he would dare to think that way.

"Of course not. I don't think you understand, comrade. It is nearly impossible to get into our secret group. The fact that I got both you and Anderson in is unprecedented. It simply isn't done because of the risks the dungeon runs with each new member, especially newbies. You have no idea how much I put on the line for you two."

"I do remember glee mentioning how unusual it was."

"Then you realize there is absolutely no way I would be allowed to bring another inexperienced member into the group."

I'm disappointed, but I completely understand. "Of course, and thank you for sticking your neck out for Anderson and me."

He shrugs one shoulder. "Eh, it was nothing."

"But you just said…"

"I was merely being polite, you peasant. I put everything on the line for you."

"Oh, there it is—that condescending attitude associated with people born into money. Fucking aristocrat," I joke.

Durov smirks. "I'd rather be an aristocrat than a peasant."

"Naturally, that's what someone born into money would say."

He socks me in the shoulder. "*Mudak.*"

"You do know I understand what that means? I haven't stopped studying Russian, asshole."

He raises his eyebrows. "Still studying my language, are you?"

"Yes. I want to be prepared for moments just like this, when you make rude comments because you think I don't know what you're saying."

"You impress me, peasant," he says with a grin, then changes the subject. "If you are serious about wanting to introduce this woman to Domination, I would suggest training her yourself."

"Me? I barely know what I am doing."

"Sometimes, the best teachers are other students, *moy droog.*"

"But, wouldn't you be a better choice?"

"I have zero interest in training others. Besides, I don't even know the woman."

"I could introduce you. She told me she's interested in meeting you."

He smirks. "Of course, she is. Still...I will not take her on."

"Fine," I answer, not hiding my disappointment.

"Has she expressed an interest in being a Domme?"

I chuckle. "Actually, she may not even know what BDSM is—much like myself when you took me to the dungeon that first time."

"What makes you think she would even be interested? Has she been topping you in the bedroom?" he asks, elbowing me in the ribs.

I roll my eyes. "It's not like that."

"What is it, then?" he demands, looking sincerely interested.

"It's just a feeling I have. I can't explain it."

"Do you have that same feeling with people you think are potential submissives?"

I raise an eyebrow. "As a matter of fact, I do."

Durov nods. "I felt the same way with you. I could sense it. If you truly feel that way about her, then I suggest training her yourself. As you learn, you can teach her."

For some reason, the idea of sharing my newfound knowledge with Samantha excites me. "I will take it under advisement, Durov."

He socks me in the arm again. "You do that, peasant."

I shake my head in warning. "You certainly know how to push my buttons."

"It's a natural ability of any sadist."

"Well, that is one thing I'm certain I'm not."

He chuckles. "You are not a masochist, either."

"No."

"What are you, then? Do you have an interest in bondage?"

"I do, but not as my sole focus."

"What is your focus then?"

I laugh. "I haven't figured that out yet."

"Well, *moy droog*," he says, placing his arm around my shoulder. "You have plenty of avenues to explore."

"It is my mission to explore them all."

"Ah…you want to be a jack of all trades, but master of none?"

"No. I want to have a wide range of skills so I never get bored."

"A pretty lofty goal, comrade."

"You believe I should specialize, then?"

"No, *moy droog*. I actually admire you ambition, not that I want that for myself."

"Why would you? I'm a peasant."

"Exactly."

"Durov…"

He chuckles. "What?"

I look at him, pausing for a moment, before saying in all seriousness, "Thank you."

Clasping me around the shoulders, he says, "No need to thank me again, *moy droog*. We were square the night you thanked me after visiting the dungeon. I just wanted to see you grovel a little because it amuses me."

*Fucking sadist…*

# A New Path

"So we're really going through with this?" I ask when I see Anderson taking out his bullwhip.

He grins as he coils it up and secures it to his belt.

"You've found a place that's secluded, right? The last thing I want is to draw a crowd like we did last time."

"Don't worry. Your crush on me will remain our little secret."

"I think that's the other way around. I didn't ask to do this," I remind him.

Anderson winks at me. "Sure, buddy."

I hit him in the shoulder as we head out the door.

It's still early in the morning and a fog covers the campus. The cold chill in the morning air invigorates me, and I find I'm actually looking forward to this little experiment in bullwhip control. I'm secretly grateful that Anderson is *not* a sadist.

The campus itself is eerily quiet except for a few dedicated joggers. Anderson leads me through the fog to a secluded area in the back of the Engineering building.

"Perfect," I tell him after I survey the place. Stripping off my shirt, I throw it at him. "Let's get this over with so we can head back to the dorm."

The caress of the cool air raises goosebumps on my skin while I wait for Anderson to warm up with his whip.

He's careful not to make it crack—neither of us wanting to draw attention to this unusual morning activity of ours. This unusual endeavor would only invite questions and speculation, which I want to avoid at all costs.

The fact that I have made it through the first semester and managed to fly under the radar is a minor miracle in itself. As far as I can tell, Durov is the only one who knows my identity. So, my plan now is to keep my head down in college, but still indulge in a little private kink on the side.

I fold my arms in front of me once he stops swinging the whip. I want to give him full access to my back while preventing accidental injury to my arms and hands. That fact is that my back can be easily covered up should Anderson prove not to be as skilled as he thinks. Knowing this is his first time using the whip on a human, I'm not taking any chances.

"I'm ready if you are," Anderson states, as he moves into position behind me.

"Let her rip."

With wisps of fog curling around me, I wait for the first lash of his bullwhip. When he lets it fly, all I feel is the brush of the cracker against my skin. The lightness of the stroke is shocking, especially after experiencing the severe pain of Durov's 'nines.

"How was that?" he asks me.

Knowing his last test subject was a cow, I answer with a long, "Moooo…"

"Very funny, smart guy."

"Try it again," I tell him in all seriousness, wanting something to compare with the first one.

After the second lash, I'm better able to answer him. "It feels as if you are holding the cracker in your hand and brushing it roughly against my skin."

"But you wouldn't describe it as a lick?"

"No."

"Let me try again, then," he tells me. After several practice throws, he gets into position. I close my eyes this time, not wanting anything to distract me.

This lash is even lighter when it brushes against my skin.

"I'd call that more of a lick."

"Okay. Let me try to repeat it."

After several more strokes of his whip, he feels confident he can deliver the same level of impact and says, "We're done here."

However, before he calls it quits I tell him, "I'd like to see if you can make it the barest whisper of a touch."

He looks at me as if I'm crazy.

But I challenge him by asking, "What's the harm in trying?"

Anderson shakes his head, running his hand through his hair. "I don't think you realize the skill it takes to deliver the lashes I just gave you."

"You're wrong. I *do* realize how skilled you are,

which is why I want you to try an even lighter touch. Any talented bullwhip Master can do what you just did, but taking it up a notch? What girl wouldn't get excited to experience something they've never felt from anyone else?"

Anderson nods. "Yeah...I'm liking that idea." He glances around and frowns. "But the fog is starting to lift. Are you sure you want to stay out here longer?"

"Give it a couple of tries. If it's too difficult, we'll call it quits."

I turn, offering my back to him, curious to see if he can impress me further.

Again, Anderson swings the whip several times, attempting to perfect an even lighter flick of the whip before testing it on me.

When he's ready, Anderson repositions himself and lets it fly.

It is lighter than the last, but I am sure he can do better. "Try again."

He strokes my back again and, while impressive, it's still not good enough. "Again."

Anderson growls in frustration but tries several more times to impress me.

"You're close," I encourage him when it seems he's about to give up.

"I'm giving you exactly what you asked for, Davis," he growls.

I honestly feel he's close and tell him, "Don't stop. You've almost got it."

I hear him take in a long breath and know he is trying to keep calm in order to maintain his level of control.

He lashes me with the whip, and I barely feel the touch of it.

"That's it!"

Anderson laughs in relief, then tries several more times until he can consistently "lick" my skin with the whip.

"Damn impressive," I tell him once he's done.

Anderson has a pleased grin on his face, boasting, "Sometimes, I amaze myself! Do you want to be really impressed?"

"Sure…" I answer uncertainly, knowing his love of pranks.

"Heads up. This might hurt if I get it wrong."

"Way to build my confidence."

"It'll be worth it. Trust me."

I'm not quite sure what I've just agreed to, but my curiosity forces me to turn my back to him once more as I watch the last of the fog clear away. We've run out of time.

I hear Anderson take a deep breath before letting it fly, perfectly placing the lash directly on one of the last remaining marks left by Durov's cat-o'-nines.

The area is still sensitive, so even the light touch of the whip carries a sting to it, but damn…I *am* impressed by his control.

Anderson quickly throws my shirt back at me as he curls up the bullwhip just as a small group of engineering students walk by.

He nods at me and says, "Let's get out of here."

I look at Anderson with greater admiration as we walk back to the dorm.

"What?" he asks, grinning.

"I guess your mama was right to praise you so highly."

His grin grows wider. "You know, I struggled not to snap you with a painful lash for pushing me so hard, but I'm glad you did. You helped me cross a mental limit I had no idea I'd set for myself."

I feel a deep sense of satisfaction knowing I've encouraged Anderson to cross that limit.

Thinking about Samantha again as I start up the long flight of stairs to the room, I decide to take Durov's suggestion. Even though the conversation may get uncomfortable, I want to see if Samantha has any interest in being a Dominant.

What's the worst that can happen?

I take Samantha to an upscale restaurant because it's known for its private dining rooms. We'll need that privacy once I start the conversation with her. I dress up for the evening and offer to pick her up, but she insists on meeting me there instead.

Once I arrive, I find Samantha is already there, waiting for me at the bar. I notice she's dressed in the same conservative apparel she wears every day at school.

When she turns around and sees my formal suit, she immediately frowns. "What? I thought this was a simple dinner between friends."

"It is," I assure her.

"Well, your formal suit says otherwise."

"Jackets are requirement at this establishment."

"Hmm…" she mutters, her frown deepening.

I wonder at the sudden change in her, and I can tell something is seriously off as we follow the hostess to our private room. I was confident about approaching her with my offer of instruction, but now…I'm not feeling so sure.

"Your server will be with you shortly," the hostess informs us, quietly shutting the door and leaving us alone together.

The silence between us takes over the room as I stare at Samantha across the table. I feel her anxiety rising as she meets my gaze.

Before my own nerves start kicking in, I tell her, "I have something important I want to ask you."

"Oh, God…" she groans. "Davis, I know exactly what you are going to say and the answer is a flat no."

"You have no idea what I am about to ask."

"This private room, the fancy suit, *and* a nice restaurant…?"

"I'm not asking you to be my girlfriend, if that's what you're worried about." I try not to laugh when I add, "But I'm truly flattered."

"Don't you even…" she huffs, standing up. Narrowing her eyes, she declares in an icy tone, "The last thing I would *ever* do is date a man who looks like my dead brother."

"Of course not," I reply soothingly.

I can see Samantha's embarrassed and is glancing at the door as if she's about to leave. This does not bode well, considering the nature of the offer I wish to discuss.

"Stay, Samantha. I never meant to upset you. I asked you here because I have something important I want to share with you."

"What's this all about?" she demands, her hands on her hips.

"I'm not trying to seduce you. That's definitely *not* what this is about."

"Then explain yourself!" she barks, looking as if she's ready to bolt at any second.

"I need you to sit back down and listen."

She stares at me warily, not moving.

"Samantha, I would never do anything to intentionally hurt or embarrass you," I assure her.

She sits back down slowly, but I can tell her defenses are still up.

"Do you remember that Russian I told you about?"

"Oh, my God. You're trying to set me up!" she cries, standing again.

"No. Sit down and let me finish," I command firmly.

She sits back down, but folds her arms in a defensive manner.

I can see this ending in disaster, but forge onward. "As I was saying, the Russian shared something with me that I've never seen or experienced before."

Her eyes narrow with distrust, and I can tell she is mentally running through every possible scenario, each one progressively worse than the last.

"Have you ever heard of BDSM?"

"What?"

I may lose a friendship over this, but explain, "BDSM is an acronym for bondage, discipline, sadism, and masochism."

"I know what it is," she snaps.

*Well, that's a surprise…*

"I even tried it," she continues. "But, I'll be damned if I'll let anyone order me around, *especially* in the bedroom."

"I actually agree. I don't see you as a submissive at all."

Her nostrils flare. "What are you trying to get at, Davis? My patience is running out."

I lean forward to emphasize the importance of what I am about to tell her. "I'm learning the fundamentals of Domination and I wondered if you would be interested in learning with me."

She just stares at me.

When she remains silent, I ask, "Have I offended you?"

Samantha leans back in her chair, uncrossing her arms. She purses her lips, thinking for a moment before replying. "What would that even look like?"

"I was planning to show you by example. I'd demonstrate with a submissive and you could then practice what you've learned."

She crinkles her brow. "Where would you find a willing submissive?"

"I've already spoken to someone who says she's willing."

"She?"

"Yes. Is that an issue for you?"

Samantha's lips slowly curl upward. "No. Not at all, actually."

"Are we a go, then?" I ask, surprised by the unexpected turn of events.

"Davis, do you really feel qualified to teach me?"

"No, but I promise whatever I learn, I'll pass on to you. There may even come a point when you are the one teaching me."

Samantha nods, now noticeably more relaxed. "I like your honest answer. I've seen far too many Doms who have a cocky attitude which makes me want to slap those irritating smirks clean off their faces."

I chuckle to myself, thinking of Durov. If these two ever meet, there would definitely be fireworks—and it wouldn't be pretty.

# Femme Fatale

I'm not exactly sure how I'm going to swing my college courses while practicing BDSM *and* teaching Samantha on the side, but I am exhilarated by the challenge.

As much as I enjoy my scenes at the dungeon, what motivates me is knowing that every experience, tool, or technique I learn will be passed on to my subs, as well as Samantha. It stirs something profound in my soul.

The act of instructing is an aphrodisiac in itself.

I am riding high, a feeling I never thought I would experience again, as I put in the extra hours needed to keep up with my studies.

Anderson has been noticing the extra hours, and pulls me to the side. "I have to say you've been burning the midnight oil for weeks now, buddy. I'm getting a little concerned for you."

"Don't be. I've finally found my balance."

"What? Working yourself to death?" Anderson asks with a snort. "You really need to take time out for yourself."

"Playing at the dungeon is my time."

"But you told me you're adding a student to the mix. I'm legitimately worried about you, man."

"Don't be. That's what I'm looking forward to the most. The idea of teaching someone else seems to invigorate me in a way not even my college classes can."

Anderson puts his arm around me, grinning. "It sounds like I'm getting closer to winning our bet."

"You may be…" I concede. "Hey, did you ever finish that chemistry paper you were talking about?"

He chuckles. "Ah, hell. I done clean forgot about it. Guess I better burn the midnight oil with you tonight."

Anderson doesn't see how easily I've led him into my web. Before this semester ends, I will make a serious scholar of him yet.

I rent a hotel for my first session with Samantha. It seems humorous, renting a room as if I'm having an illicit affair, but I need a private place to instruct Samantha, and a dorm room won't do.

I plan to keep this first session very basic, focusing on the dynamic of Dominance and submission. I firmly believe the mental aspect of the power exchange is the real allure of BDSM.

While Samantha insists on meeting me there, glee is grateful when I offer to pick her up. When I arrive at glee's place, I get out of the taxi to open the door for her.

Glee looks at me shyly. "You don't have to do that for me, Sir."

"Yes, I do," I correct her. "You are doing me a considerable favor tonight."

She smiles up at me. "But it is my pleasure, Sir."

Once we're on the road, I notice glee seems to be anxious and ask in a low voice so the cabbie can't hear, "Are you nervous about tonight?"

"No, not really."

"A little?" I press.

She gives me a half-smile. "I've never been in a situation like this before. I've scened with two Doms, and I've served under both Doms and Dommes, but to be part of a lesson? It holds so much more gravity."

I brush my hand against her cheek. I appreciate the fact that she feels as invested as I do. "The only thing I ask is that you respond naturally, and remain completely open and honest."

She blushes. "Even if I have something critical to say?" Glee rolls her eyes upward, shaking her head. "The thought of critiquing a Dominant, even a newbie, freaks me out."

I look at her, admiring her even more for her kind heart. "This is not a typical situation. We are here to instruct. Therefore, your critiques are vital."

She nods but still looks unsure of herself.

"Glee, the only thing required of you is your honesty. I want you to understand the profound value of it."

She looks into my eyes and smiles, saying quietly, "Thank you, Sir."

I kiss her on the forehead. "I'm grateful for you joining me in this new venture."

I hide my anxiety as I check us in under false names and pay in cash, not wanting anyone to know who we are. I let the desk clerk know I have another woman joining us and, being in LA, the clerk doesn't even bat an eye, asking, "What does she look like?"

"Tall woman. Long, blonde hair."

"I believe she's already stopped by the desk. She mentioned she would be waiting at the entrance."

I'm surprised I didn't see Samantha, but thank the clerk before I go in search of her. I order glee to remain at the check-in desk while I locate her.

Returning to the entrance, I still don't see Samantha. It isn't until I scan the lobby that I catch her coming out of the restroom. I can tell by the way she keeps touching her lips to check her lipstick that she's nervous. Her eyes dart around the lobby apprehensively, but as soon as she sees me, she straightens her back and lifts her chin, walking over with practiced confidence.

I'm actually relieved to know she is feeling as nervous as I am. It's a natural response to anything unknown but, as a Dominant, it is important to exude inner confidence. The trick, however, lies in not letting that confidence interfere when a scene isn't working.

I'd recently heard a story about a Dominant new to bondage who honored the wishes of a submissive he was pursuing. She wanted to be suspended with rope. He had no business granting her request, having only witnessed suspension bondage himself, but he agreed anyway, hoping to win her devotion. Unfamiliar with human anatomy, he unknowingly cut off the blood supply to several parts of her body with poor rope placement and ended up causing permanent nerve damage.

He admitted to another Dom afterward that his overconfidence had gotten the best of him. Even though he felt uneasy several times during the scene, he'd ignored the feeling because he wanted to impress her.

His need to impress ended up crippling her for life.

Several Doms at the dungeon have shared with me that even after performing a scene numerous times, there's always the chance of things going wrong. However, an experienced Dom will end the scene and face the sub's disappointment.

I've personally vowed to be as honest with myself as I expect my subs to be. If something isn't working, I will end it rather than risk the safety of my sub—or myself.

Of course, that is *not* going to be an issue with this first lesson. However, moving forward, I believe it's an important topic to address with Samantha. I will not train someone who refuses to put safety before ego.

When Samantha reaches me, she smiles confidently. "Davis."

"Are you ready for your first lesson?"

She glances around, and then eyes me with suspicion. "Where's the sub?"

I chuckle, knowing she still harbors fears that I have an ulterior motive.

"Glee is over there," I answer, pointing to her. "Let me introduce you."

When glee sees us approaching, she bows her head slightly rather than kneeling, so as not to attract the attention of others.

"Glee, it's my pleasure to introduce Ms. Clark to you."

"It's an honor," she replies, giving Samantha another small head bow out of respect.

Samantha looks her over and smiles. "I see that Davis has extremely good taste in submissives."

Glee glances up at her briefly, her cheeks coloring before looking back down at the floor. I can already see there's chemistry between them which will make this evening go even more smoothly. While chemistry with a sub is not essential to a scene, it definitely adds to the enjoyment of it for all parties involved.

As we head up in the elevator, the three of us are silent as we each contemplate what's about to happen. The minute I step into the hotel room, however, I stop being Samantha's friend and take on the role as her instructor.

"Glee has graciously volunteered her time tonight to help me demonstrate the concepts I will be covering. I feel seeing firsthand what is being taught, then applying what you've learned, will help cement the concepts for you."

*That's my plan, at least...*

Samantha nods. "I can see the value in that."

I explain to her that my focus for tonight's lesson is on the power exchange itself, then proceed to share what

I have learned and experienced thus far. It's not just for her benefit, but for glee's, as well. I want both women to feel comfortable with where the night's curriculum is headed.

"Now that I've covered the basics of the power exchange, let me demonstrate how that plays out at the beginning of a scene."

I turn to face glee, telling Samantha. "I want her to undress, but there are several ways I can accomplish this and each one will invoke a distinctive response from your sub. Observe…"

Addressing glee, I explain to her, "I'm going to give you a command, but I don't want you to follow through with the action. I only need you to tell me how it makes you feel after you hear it."

"Yes, Sir," glee replies, swallowing nervously.

She has done countless scenes with extremely demanding Doms, but it's her feeling of responsibility toward Samantha that has her concerned and anxious—and I cherish glee all the more for it.

"Glee, please undress for me."

She looks at me questioningly.

"How did that make you feel?"

She blushes when she answers. "It makes me feel like you're not very confident. That wasn't a command. It was a request."

"Exactly."

I bark out my next command. "Strip, *now*!"

"That's very commanding, Sir. It lets me know we're heading straight into the scene."

I move over to her, fisting her hair and kissing her

deeply before growling in her ear, "Bare yourself to me."

She purrs. "Sexy *and* commanding…"

Changing tactics, I scowl at her. "Strip, bitch, like the whore you are."

"Oh, I know I'm going to experience a humiliation scene with that command." She smiles at Samantha. "And, I happen to enjoy those, so that's hot for me."

Moving in closer to her, I command huskily, "Look at me while you undress."

"That's intimate, Sir," she says breathlessly. "Makes me feel vulnerable…in a good way."

I turn back to Samantha. "It's important to be conscious of your words and the tone of your voice. I believe every word spoken during a scene should reflect the emotion you want your submissive to experience."

Samantha nods, her lips curling into a smile.

"Now, imagine if simple words can have that kind of effect on your sub, how important every look, every touch—even a simple pause—can be? I'm a firm believer that before you dominate the body, you must *first* dominate the mind."

I'm encouraged by the excitement and understanding I see in Samantha's eyes. "Any questions?"

"No, please go on," she insists.

It's seems as if Samantha is soaking up everything I tell her—and I find it almost as exhilarating as performing BDSM itself.

"Obviously, it's important to have a conversation with the submissive beforehand, unless you already have a well-established history together. In this case, I know two things about glee that I will share with you. She is a masochist and she enjoys having marks."

I turn toward glee and she smiles up at me. "Yes. I do, Sir."

"Asking permission to leave marks is a must," I inform Samantha. "Consent is key."

Turning back to glee, I ask, "Do I have permission to leave marks on you tonight?"

"You do, Sir."

I explain to Samantha, "As I stated earlier, the lesson tonight focuses on the power exchange, so we will be utilizing a very simple technique this evening."

I turn back to glee. "I want to bite you. It may be on the neck, your shoulders, the fleshy part of your chest, or even your ass. Are you agreeable?"

Her eyes widen in excitement. "Yes, please!"

I look back to Samantha. "By asking, I have accomplished two things. I now have her consent *and* I have glee anticipating what I am about to do, but not knowing exactly where I plan to bite her."

"You are a canny one, Davis," Samantha states with admiration.

I correct her on my name, letting her know I prefer to be called Sir Davis when we work together like this.

She raises her eyebrows. "Okay...Sir Davis."

"And how would you like to be addressed?"

Samantha looks at glee and a slow smile plays on her lips. "You may call me Ms. Clark, Sir Davis. But you," she tells glee, "will call me Mistress."

Glee bows her head. "Yes, Mistress."

"Oh, I like the sound of that coming from her lips," Samantha tells me. If it wasn't obvious before, it is now—she was made to play the role of a Dominant.

"As with anything you do to your sub, you should understand how to bite safely if you want to leave marks. It's important to know the safe areas to bite and the right pressure to apply to get the mark you desire. The aim is not to break the skin, but to bruise it. The level of bruising is up to you, once you've perfected the technique. For the greatest impact on your sub, you'll want to find the bite."

"Find the bite?" Samantha asks.

I look at glee and smile as I answer.

"You want to explore her body with your mouth. Start with kissing, then slowly up the pressure of your teeth on her skin with light nibbles. When she gives you a response by either moaning or leaning into your mouth, you know you have located a good spot to bite deeper. Sink your teeth in and slowly up the intensity as you let your sub get used to it. If they start pulling away, that's your cue to back off a bit."

I turn to glee and find her looking at me lustfully. Apparently, the thought of my biting her has the little sub excited.

With my gaze still on glee, I tell Samantha, "For simplicity's sake, I will concentrate on her throat for this demonstration."

I turn glee's head to the side and lower my mouth to her neck. The instant my lips touch her skin, I feel her tremble slightly. Her instinctual reaction is a turn-on for me.

I move in and start lightly kissing the area I want to mark. I build up the sensual tension as I nibble on that tender area of her throat.

Her subtle sounds of pleasure let me know I have a perfect location. Like a lion, I take possession of her as I start biting her throat harder.

I feel glee tense up while her moaning grows louder. There is a heightened feeling of power as I continue to increase the pressure and feel her move into the bite. Grasping her neck, I bite even harder, knowing my teeth are bruising her skin.

Her passionate sighs of pleasure are erotic, adding to the intimacy of my simple embrace. When I pull away, I look down with satisfaction at the teeth marks I've left behind.

"Oh, Sir..." she whispers, encouraging me to continue.

As much as I want to, this demonstration is not for me, so I turn to Samantha. "Are you ready to play out a short scene with glee utilizing what you've learned tonight?"

"Could I have a few minutes to play it out in my mind before I start?"

"Of course. I expect you to plan out the scene mentally in order to accomplish the goal you wish to achieve."

Samantha stands up and begins pacing the room as she works out what she wants to do with glee.

I notice glee watching Samantha intently. I'm curious how this scene will play out between the two. To make sure my libido doesn't get the better of me while I observe them, I remind myself of my role here.

When Samantha turns and states that she's ready, I

notice a change in her. Instead of an interested student, I see a woman ready to take charge.

I sit down to observe, determined not to interfere unless I'm needed. I want Samantha to own this scene.

She walks over to glee and commands, "Bow to me."

Glee immediately kneels on the floor.

"As I said before, you will address me as Mistress."

Keeping her head down, glee answers, "Yes, Mistress."

"I want you to take all your clothes off and turn around slowly several times so I can admire your naked body."

I smile to myself, appreciating the initial tone she has set for the scene.

Glee stands up and quickly undresses, setting her clothes to the side. As ordered, glee begins spinning slowly for Samantha, who looks on her lustfully.

When glee stops after several turns, Samantha tells her, "Keep spinning. I'm deciding where to bite you."

Glee's face lights up as she slowly turns again for Samantha.

"Stop," she orders when glee is facing away from her. Samantha grazes her skin with her long fingernails. Taking heed of my instruction, Samantha does not rush as she runs her hands over glee's body.

After exploring her through touch, Samantha orders glee to lie down on the bed, building up the anticipation.

Glee looks up at Samantha expectantly as she lies down. I can see by Samantha's expression that she is now fully realizing and appreciating the power she wields over glee. It seems to be as intoxicating for her as it was for me my first time.

Samantha begins exploring glee with her lips, being thorough as she tests every sensitive spot, drawing out her exploration while she finds the area where she wants to leave her mark.

Glee is totally invested, squirming and moaning whenever Samantha finds another sensual area to mark. By the time she is done, Samantha has located at least five and left glee wondering which one she will choose.

*Brilliant.*

Lying down beside her, Samantha reaches between her legs and begins stroking her clit lightly as she leaves a trail of light kisses over glee's chest. What starts out slow and sensual soon becomes hotter when her fingers begin moving at a more rapid pace.

I watch glee respond to her, spreading her legs wider as her pussy gets wetter and more swollen from Samantha's concentrated attention.

Soon she is arching her back and panting loudly.

Samantha takes the cue, leaning down and sinking her teeth in just above glee's nipple. Taking her time, she draws out the bite by slowly increasing the pressure of her teeth, causing glee to cry out in desire.

When glee begins squirming with pleasure, Samantha surprises her by slapping her pussy hard with the palm of her hand.

Glee momentary freezes from the unexpected shock, then begins moaning even louder when Samantha begins stimulating her clit again as she bites down hard.

I watch as glee's hips rise in the air and her pussy begin pulsing rhythmically as she comes.

Afterward, Samantha raises her head and I see the mark she's left behind. The indents of her teeth are deep and clear, but the skin is left unbroken.

Samantha leans in and kisses glee on the lips. "Now you have something to remember me by."

I see the look of admiration in glee's eyes when she answers, "Yes, Mistress."

As they lay there together, basking in the success of their scene, I feel a deep sense of accomplishment. Not only did the lesson go off without a hitch, but Samantha has also proven herself an intuitive Domme.

I feel strongly that she will do well in this environment and it may prove as life changing for her as it has been for me.

Samantha glances over at me and frowns slightly.

"What?" I ask, wondering what's wrong.

"You look different with your guard down."

I don't know what she means and immediately dismiss it, until glee agrees.

"You look…at ease, Sir. It's very becoming on you."

I laugh it off, but the truth is, I have a feeling of inner satisfaction that I haven't experienced before. "This is the perfect stopping point for the lesson tonight. Glee, when you are ready, clean yourself up and dress. I'll take you home."

After she leaves the room, Samantha asks, "So, Sir Davis, when is our next lesson?"

Watching Samantha as she took on the role of a Domme, I saw a whole new woman emerging. It is a heady feeling witnessing the transformation and knowing I've had a part in it.

"I'm unsure at this point, but I'll let you know."

"As long as there's another, I can be patient."

"You did well today, Samantha."

She looks down at the floor, smiling, but when she meets my gaze again, I'm struck by her vulnerability. She whispers, "Thanks."

Taking two stairs at a time, I head up to the dorm room, anxious to tell Anderson how successful the night has been. I burst into our room and instantly stop in my tracks.

The room is dark and empty, but the hairs on the back of my neck start to rise.

I know that smell...

A paralyzing sense of dread takes over as remnants of *her* perfume linger in the air—taunting me.

# Master of Lies

Before I can recover from the shock, Anderson comes barging into the room. He glares at me, growling, "What the fucking hell, man?"

I quickly shut the door. "You've got it all wrong."

"You bet I do. Because all this time you've been lying to me. Fucking asshole! You had me believing your mother was dead—but she's not. She's very much alive."

I shake my head violently, horrified that she's forced herself back into my life.

"You're a dick, *Thane*. And yes, she told me your fucking name." He walks over to me, getting all up in my face. "I thought we were friends, but I don't even know who you are."

I concentrate on taking deep breaths, so I don't release the all-consuming rage I've suppressed for the last two years on my friend.

Anderson stares at me, his gaze full of shock and disappointment. "A real man doesn't treat his own *mother* that way, especially after what happened with your father."

I'm finding it more and more difficult to breathe, and the rage only builds when I hear him mention my father in the same breath as the Beast.

"How did she get to you?" I demand.

"Your mother came looking for you, *buddy.*" He bites out the last word disdainfully. "And, damn, you should have seen the tears when she learned you told me she was dead. It wasn't right for you to put me in that position."

"Where is she now?" I insist, my heart racing with anger and fear.

*She's going to ruin everything…*

Anderson puts his hand on his chest. "I did right by your poor mama by taking her out for dinner." He glares at me. "I've never seen a woman so brokenhearted—so many damn tears. I understand now why you're so shifty about your past. You have a lot to atone for."

I'm royally fucked. I know firsthand the kind of damage she's capable of. "Anderson, you can't believe a word she says," I warn him. "The Beast is the master of lies."

He points his finger at me, digging it into my chest. "You better not ever call your mother that again in my presence."

I shake my head in disbelief, stunned that she's already managed to turn Anderson against me. Staring at him in shock, I'm unable to hide the intense hatred I'm feeling for her.

"Yeah, that look you're giving me right now—that's the real you. She warned me I would see it," Anderson informs me.

With more control than I knew I possessed, I make no move toward him, growling through gritted teeth, "Stop defending the Beast."

He cocks his fist back to hit me but stops himself just before making contact. Instead, he hisses with disgust, "I can't even stand to look at you."

Anderson slams the door so hard, the entire room shakes from the force of it. The silence that follows is deadly.

I close my eyes as a chilling numbness overtakes me...

Now that I know she's here, I can't get the taint of her out of my mind. Being alone only makes it worse.

I seek out the Russian and find him playing pool with the guys at his dorm. "Durov," I call out, my voice shaking with anger.

He's bent over the table, about to take a shot, but as soon as he hears my voice, he looks up and instantly lowers his pool stick. Without saying a word, he hands it to one of the guys. Grabbing my arm, he walks me outside.

"I can see you are seething with rage." He spreads his arms out. "Go ahead, hit me."

I stare at him, frowning. "I'm not going to hit you."

"It will help release the negative energy. Trust me."

After several proddings, and against my better

judgement, I hit him halfheartedly in the chest. He immediately follows it up with a hard jab to my gut.

My instinctual reaction is to hit him in the face, bloodying his nose.

Durov smiles at me like a crazy person before he lets loose. The two of us fight, hitting each other over and over until we are both bloody—and I have no fight left in me.

I fall to the ground, spent and panting for breath.

Durov sits down beside me and bumps my shoulder. "What is wrong, *moy droog?*"

"My…"—I struggle to say the word—"…mother is here."

"I know."

I look at him with concern. "How? Did she come to you?"

"*Da.*"

Unlike Anderson, he does not seem upset by the encounter. "What happened?"

"The woman accosted me outside the cafeteria after my evening meal."

"When you say accosted, what do you mean?"

"She was teary-eyed and sniveling outside the cafeteria when she called out my name. I did not recognize who she was." Durov adds with a smirk, "So, naturally, I stopped to speak with such a beautiful woman."

I swallow down the fear growing in my heart, knowing the fatal affect her beauty has on men. "What did she say to you?"

"The woman claimed she was looking for you and asked if I knew where you were. Not being a trusting soul, I demanded to know exactly who she was. When I heard she was your mother, I was tempted to escort her to your dorm, remembering our conversation about how much you loved her."

I cringe, remembering that conversation. I wasn't forthright with Durov then, and now I'm living to regret it. "But, how the hell did she know who you were in the first place?"

"I wanted to know that myself, comrade. When I asked her, I learned she had already spoken to Anderson."

I feel the air leave my lungs and wonder how much she was able to weasel out of an unsuspecting Anderson over the course of an entire meal.

*This is my fault…*

In wanting to protect myself by not speaking of her, I've left everyone I've grown close to vulnerable to the Beast. I should have known that even a restraining order wouldn't stop her.

The ugly reality is that as long as she lives, I will always be at her mercy.

*I will never know peace.*

Durov continues, "When she started whining about your betrayal and pressing me for more information, I knew what I was dealing with."

A spark of hope suddenly rises within me. "What?"

"A traitor."

Tears prick my eyes as I whisper hoarsely, "Yes…"

"It was then that I remembered whenever you spoke of her, it was always in the past tense. A man doesn't do that unless the person has died in their heart. I, myself, have known such betrayal."

I want to hug the bloody Russian. "What did you end up telling her?"

"I called her a whore, and that I would see her in hell."

I let out strained laughter, imagining the expression on her face.

Durov slaps me hard on the back. "You are like a brother to me, *moy droog*—I will never betray you."

I accept what's happened is partly my fault. Anderson trusted me without question, but I didn't trust him enough to be entirely honest.

I can't blame him for feeling betrayed, but it still hurts when I return and find his bed empty. I need to talk this out before her words worm their way into his mind so deeply that he won't be able to hear the truth.

My mother is effectively cruel.

I can only imagine what my father felt the day he died.

Feeling the need to check on Samantha, I give her a quick call. It goes through to her answering machine and I am forced to leave a message.

I have a bad feeling about Samantha. My mother has the ungodly ability to pinpoint a person's weakness and chip away at it with deadly precision.

I cannot let her hurt my friends.

Rather than worry about her, I decide to act. Even

though it's after hours, I head to Samantha's dorm and wait until an opportunity presents itself to make my way inside without being noticed.

I take the stairs to her floor, taking care to avoid detection since males are not allowed in the building after ten PM.

After waiting several minutes in the stairwell for a conversation to play out in the hall, I approach Samantha's door and knock softly.

I hear her broken voice on the other side. "Who is it?"

"It's me."

I hear her walk to the door, but she doesn't open it. "Leave."

"Did a woman claiming to be my mother contact you?"

"You can stop with the games. I know who you are."

"Samantha...don't let that woman get into your head."

"I hate you, Thane."

I cringe on hearing my given name because it means my mother has gotten to her. Laying my hand on the door, I warn her, "Don't listen to the lies you've been fed."

With a voice full of venom, she growls, "Every one of them came from you. How dare you take advantage of my loss! If you don't leave right now, I'm calling campus security."

I'm shocked at how thoroughly my mother has entangled herself in a matter of a few hours. I suspect she's been spying on me and planning this for days, with the sole intent of stripping away the people closest to me.

That's why I need Samantha to hear the truth before I leave tonight. "I may have kept my past from you. But, Samantha, I meant it when I told you I would never do anything to intentionally hurt you."

I hear her whimper on the other side of the door. "Why did I believe you?"

I hear her move away from the door just as the ding of the elevator alerts me that time has run out.

I head back down the stairs, facing the very real possibility that my mother may have caused irreparable damage.

When I enter my dorm room, I find Anderson has returned, but he has his back to me and his headphones on. I know he doesn't want to talk, but his friendship means too much to let this go.

I put my hand on his back, but he shrugs it off. I place it there again until he finally turns and pulls off his headphones, clearly irritated.

When he sees me, however, he instantly blurts, "What the hell happened? Finally got what you deserve?"

I'd forgotten what I must look like after the fight I'd had with Durov, but I ignore the comment without explaining. "We're talking this out."

"What? You want to have a heart-to-heart *now*? Because that's what I thought we had until I found out you that are a fucking liar…and worse."

"What do you mean by that?"

His eyes narrow. "I know what you did. What your mother is trying to hide."

I snarl. "*What I did?*"

The fucking nerve of her!

"What exactly did the Beast tell you?"

Anderson growls angrily. "I told you to stop calling her that. You can quit with your fucking act now." He lowers his voice and says ominously, "I know what really happened."

I fold my arms, staring him down. "What?"

"Your mother has been covering things up to protect you."

The Beast never protected me. No, she threw me under the bus to protect herself. I cannot, and I *will* not, lose his friendship because of her.

"I need you to hear me out," I insist. "She's had her chance to spew *her* version of his death, so I'm asking you to hear mine."

His frown deepens. "You've had all year to tell me your version."

"I know I made a mistake by keeping it from you, but she is the reason I've been hiding my identity."

"You can talk all you want, but you've lost all credibility with me."

"Whether you chose to believe me or not, you should know the truth." I pause for a moment. This is something I've never shared with another soul, not even Durov. "If you've followed their history in the news, you'd know my parents were happily married for many years—I can attest to that. They considered a golden couple, my father compared to the sun and my mother the moon. They were adored by the media and music lovers alike. But there came a point, when I was eleven or twelve, when it seemed like something snapped inside my mother. She changed, became colder and more distant toward my father…and me.

"Instead of being proud of my father's talent as a violinist, she suddenly became resentful and jealous of him. First that resentment was directed toward his travel schedule, then it turned into jealousy toward his fame until paranoia took over and she became convinced he was being unfaithful."

"He *was* unfaithful," Anderson interjects. "She showed me the proof."

"The proof she manufactured for the media after his death, hoping to gain sympathy from the world in order to distance herself from the guilt she was carrying."

Anderson folds his arms, clearly not convinced.

It's insulting not to be believed when this is so important, but I forge on for both our sakes. "It was my mother who changed—not my father. I never doubted his love for her. But the truth is, my mother had been having affairs for two years before his suicide. When I accidently walked in and discovered her betrayal, she insisted I keep quiet.

Anderson interjects, "The way I heard it, you knew of his multiple affairs, but you kept silent to protect him."

I snort in disgust. "Typical. She's stays close enough to the truth for it to be plausible but reverses the blame to show herself in a good light."

The numbness of my father's loss returns as we continue to talk.

My father is dead.

I will never see him again in this lifetime.

And, *she* is the reason he killed himself that day.

I shake my head, trying desperately to keep the visions of his death from replaying in my head.

"Anderson, understand this. As far as I'm concerned, she's to blame for his suicide. Her actions killed him even though *he* was the one who pulled the trigger."

Thinking out loud, I admit, "I should have told my father when it first happened. I knew what she was doing was wrong but, ultimately, I chose to keep silent because I wanted to protect our family."

I see a sliver of sympathy in his eyes.

"I don't know what to believe…" he mutters. "Either story could be true, but you *purposely* lied to me to keep me in the dark. Those seem like the actions of a guilty man."

I look at Anderson, the guilt associated with my father's death a constant weight on my shoulders. "Maybe I *am* partly to blame for his suicide because I didn't tell him what was happening. But I was only a thirteen-year-old kid trying to keep his family intact."

Anderson shakes his head. "You are seriously fucking with my head. I need time to figure this out." I watch him grab a duffle bag and throw some of his clothes into it.

"Anderson, I have a restraining order against her, and I can prove it." I start rummaging through my desk.

"Don't bother, Davis. I wouldn't believe it even if

you showed me....I'm out of here." Before he leaves, he stops to look back at me. "Either you deserve my deepest sympathy or you're a crazy fuck and deserve another punch in the face."

I find myself alone again. Wiping the dried blood from my lip, I sit down at my desk and pull out a textbook from the stack. I was a fool to think I could make a life outside of my mother's influence—I shouldn't have even bothered.

A thought suddenly comes to me, causing goosebumps to rise on my skin.

*What if I end up like my father?*

# Reclaiming What's Mine

Too exhausted to keep my eyes open any longer, I finally head to bed. The room has a completely different feel to it now that Anderson isn't here, and I find I can't sleep.

I lay on my back with my headphones on, listening to the lonely sound of my father's violin. It feels as if I am hearing his voice as the violin sings its forlorn melody. I haven't listened to his music since the suicide, knowing how much it would hurt me to hear it.

But tonight, I take solace in the emotional connection as my tears fall unheeded.

"*Papà*...I hear you."

I hover between the states of reality and sleep, and in that dreamlike place, my father's music takes on a more familiar tone, blending and transforming into his voice...

"You've almost got it, Thane. Trim that sail."

My memories drift back to when I was eight. I'm out on the ocean with my father, sailing near the Italian island of *Isola d'Elba*, where his family lives in the town of Portoferraio. He loves to sail and always finds time to take me out on his boat whenever we visit his parents.

I love the freedom I feel when I'm on the ocean, but it's these uninterrupted times alone with my father that I cherish most. All the pressures he carries as a world-famous musician melt away when we're sailing and it's just my father and me.

"Do you see that small, deserted island over there?" he asks, pointing to a small speck on the horizon.

I raise my hand to shield my eyes from the sun and look in the direction he's pointing.

"I do, *Papà*!"

"What say you and I go claim it?"

The thrill of playing explorers has my young heart racing. "What should we call it?"

He smiles at me as he adjusts the sails. "I think you should have the honors."

I stare at the tiny island as we draw closer, already thinking of it as mine. "I'm calling it Isola d' Thane."

My father laughs. "Isola d'Thane it is, then."

He lowers the anchor once we're close enough to shore. Stripping off his shirt, he kicks off his shoes and dives into the water. I follow suit, swimming quickly to catch up with him.

Feeling like a true explorer, I climb a small cliff of rocks and look out with pride onto a grassy expanse surrounded by trees and vegetation.

My father puts his hand on my shoulder. "This is a fine island, son."

"Sí, *Papà*," I agree proudly.

Pretending it's really mine, I explore every inch of it, hoping to find buried treasure with my father. We search every outcropping of rock, and the base of the trees, as well as the sandy alcoves.

I'm so entranced by the island that I don't even care when we don't find anything. "I could live here," I declare.

My father laughs. The sound of his laughter is low and warm like the sun on my young soul.

*I've forgotten that…*

"Sorry, my boy, but that would not be very fair to your mother. You know how much she loves you."

I frown, crossing my arms in protest. I don't want to leave.

"Let's return next year to see if any pirates have left treasure behind. You and I will make it our yearly quest."

My eyes light up. "Next time, I'll bring a flag to claim the island."

Papa ruffles my hair. "And I'll stand by your side to watch you plant it."

"Promise, *Papà*?"

"Promise."

I look over Isola d'Thane with a sense of great pride, having no idea how important this small island will become to him—and me.

I drift to sleep afterward and wake up in the morning with that memory and the sound of his voice still lingering in my head.

I have hundreds of cherished memories of my father; memories I've held back because of the pain they cause. I'm realizing now that in refusing to embrace them, I have kept him at a distance and, if I continue long enough, I will lose him completely.

My father's zest for life and his contagious spirit of adventure was something I've always admired, and both live on inside me. It gives me a sense of power.

I will not concede defeat to the Beast—I need to fight for what's mine.

I go to our Advanced Economics class, hoping to speak with Samantha. When she shows up, she sees me and chooses to sit as far away as physically possible. She won't even look in my direction.

Inspired by the unexplainable sense of hope I felt earlier; I have a stroke of inspiration. Tearing out a piece of paper from my notebook, I write in large letters: *As my friend, I made a vow to never hurt you. That remains true. ~Thane*

I fold it into an airplane and write *Open me* on the left wing.

With five minutes left before class begins, feeling slightly foolish, I turn around to face her, taking aim. With a quick flick of the wrist, I send it sailing straight toward her.

Turning around quickly, I pull out my textbook and open it up to today's topic of discussion. I spend the entire class wondering if Samantha picked it up, if she read it and, if she did, what she's thinking.

When class ends, I look back at Samantha and find her staring at me but, as soon as our eyes meet, she immediately glances away.

I know I can't force her trust, and I have no idea what lies my mother has told her, so I get up and leave—giving her the space she needs.

As I head outside and start toward the grassy commons in the middle of campus, I hear her come up behind me.

"Davis!"

Despite her cold tone, I turn around, grateful she is speaking to me.

Her jaw drops. "What the hell happened to your face?"

I rub the bruise on my right cheek. "I needed to vent last night."

For a second, I see a look of concern in her eyes, but she quickly shakes if off, holding up the note. "What's the meaning of this?"

"I need you to know I keep my promises."

"So, you thought throwing a paper airplane at me in class was a good idea?"

I shrug, "I wanted to get your attention without being overly aggressive."

She shakes her head, frowning. "You scare me…"

"Why?"

I'm concerned, hearing that she feels that way.

"You're either a genuinely nice guy or evil to the core."

"I'm not a nice guy, but I'm also not a monster, Samantha. What exactly did my mother say to you?"

Samantha looks at me with a mixture of fear and distrust, but answers, "She warned me that she believes you've been using my brother's likeness to gain my trust in order to blackmail my family."

"Why would I do that?" I ask incredulously.

"She told me you're broke and that you'll do anything for money."

I snort in disgust. "It's true that I have no money, but she's the reason why."

Samantha shifts uncomfortably. "Thane, after the things we did at the hotel last night, I can't help but wonder if your sudden offer to train me was really just a set up for blackmail."

Leave it to my mother to trash my reputation and steal something positive in my life. Fuck the Beast, I'm not letting her take this from me, too.

Looking Samantha in the eyes, I tell her in no uncertain terms, "I would *never* do such a thing."

I know the accusation my mother leveled against me is seriously messing with her mind, so I ask the only question that can cut through all the lies. "What does your gut tell you, Samantha?"

She takes a deep breath before meeting my gaze again. "I trust you…." I can see that she sincerely wants to trust me, but my similarity to her brother is making her doubt her feelings now, after hearing my mother's unfounded accusation.

The Beast's deception is brilliant and cruel.

The guilt I feel for not being able to protect Samantha from that woman's influence eats at me. "I'm sorry you've become involved."

"Thane, can you tell me why a mother would say such horrible things about her own son?"

"My mother has an agenda. I don't know what it is this time." I growl under my breath. "But she *always* has an agenda and is meticulously thorough in her execution. I suspect that once she identified who you were, she investigated you, so she not only knew about your brother's death, but my likeness to him. She then weaved a story around it that would leave you open to her vicious lie."

"Oh, my God, do you think she knows what we were doing at the hotel last night?" she whispers, a look of horror on her face.

"No, she was interrogating my friend Anderson at the time. I am certain of that."

Personally, I'm grateful now that I'd taken a cab last night and didn't register under our real names at the hotel. It seems my general distrust of people proved to be an asset in this instance.

Samantha closes her eyes, breathing a sigh of relief.

I pull out the restraining order I've been carrying since discovering the Beast has found me. "I mistakenly believed this would be enough to stop her, but it's useless if she goes after the people around me."

Samantha takes the paper from me and unfolds it. "You actually have a restraining order against your mother?" As she reads it, I see a distinct change come over her.

Samantha looks up at me afterward, her eyes flashing with anger. "Your mother is a total psycho."

"Yes."

"So, let me get this straight. She fucked with me last night, just to fuck with you? That bitch needs be stopped."

Grateful my friendship with Samantha remains strong, I wait for Anderson to return, but I know with each day that passes there's a chance my mother is poisoning him with more lies.

A few days later, I'm relieved to hear from the guys at my dorm that Anderson has been looking for me. When I finally spot him outside the library, I call out his name. He turns and comes barreling toward me with a menacing look on his face. I prepare myself to be socked in the face but, when he reaches me, instead of a punch, he crushes me in a bear hug.

Squeezing the air out of me like a boa constrictor, he whispers gruffly, "I saw her again."

I tense, wondering what the next few seconds hold for me.

When he lets go, Anderson looks at me with pity. "You're so fucked."

"What do you mean?"

"That woman is certifiable."

I let out an inward sigh of relief, knowing he's on my side. "Yes, she absolutely is."

He snarls ominously. "She had the nerve to approach me again. She told me she felt compelled to share the secret she's been keeping to protect you."

"What secret?"

He glances around before saying under his breath, "Your dear old mom claims you shot your father, but she made it look like a suicide to protect you."

The blood drains from my face. Her lie is beyond anything I could ever imagine.

Anderson continues, "She must have sensed I was teetering on the fence about you, and thought she needed to implicate you further."

Knowing how Anderson and I left it the last time we talked, I ask him, "Why didn't you believe her this time?"

He runs his hand through his hair. "It makes no sense. Why would a kid kill his dad for fucking another woman? Scream at him, and punch the crap out of him, I get. But there's no reason a kid would go so far as to kill the guy. Maybe the mom would want to, but the kid? No way."

He looks at me with concern. "When I called her on it, she started crying." He shakes his head. "Damn, that woman can cry." Spitting on the ground in disgust, he tells me, "She then decided to tell me the *real* truth. Between her exaggerated sobs, she shared how your father abused you both for years."

I grab onto the bike rail beside me, needing its support. Her lies about him stab me in the heart.

After my father's suicide, she completely trashed his reputation by leaking to the media that he'd been having multiple affairs. In a matter of weeks, the world went from mourning the death of the great violinist, Alonzo Davis, to hating him for being a manwhore because of those vicious lies.

I will *never* forgive her for that.

"I'm worried about you, man. What if she tells that crap to the police?"

I pull the restraining order out of my pocket and show it to him. "Pretty sure the cops won't listen to her."

He shakes his head in disbelief. "So, you really *do* have one." Anderson looks it over, frowning. "Why didn't you tell me the truth about your mother before of all this happened?"

I let out a long sigh. "I suffered through a living hell after my father's death. People are so quick to believe the lies reported in the news…" I turn away from him, trying to regain control of my raging emotions. "I wasn't willing to deal with it again."

He slugs me in the arm. "Well, I forgive you for keeping me in the dark about her, and I hope you can forgive me for the shit that went down between us."

I turn around to face him. "There's nothing to forgive." I slug him back; grateful we have restored our trust in one another. I vow never to compromise it again.

"Hey, Davis."

"Yeah?"

"Let's bring the Beast down."

Because Rytsar immediately saw through her ruse, and Anderson let her know he's no longer buying her crap, I ask Samantha if she will act as my decoy.

"Sure, I'd love to get even with her. What do you need me to do?"

"It's a given my mother will be seeking you out now that she's made contact. She's been strategic about stalking me without breaking the restraining order. However, I have a plan to work around that..."

What the Beast fails to realize is that I *am* her son, and I can be equally ruthless when threatened.

# Going Down

It upsets Samantha to no end that my mother used her. "What's wrong with me?"

"Don't beat yourself up over it," I tell her. "The Beast had the element of surprise and utilized it to her full advantage after pumping information out of Anderson."

"But Thane, I'm not a gullible person. I don't trust people, in general. And yet, that woman was able to make me question everything about you, and I'd never even met her before. Hell, she could have been *anybody*." Samantha looks at me sadly, as she takes a sip of her coffee. "You didn't deserve that."

"Fortunately, I understand how she operates, so I'm not offended. I just wish I'd been able to protect you from her. The Beast is extremely skillful at tapping into a person's insecurities. I'm relieved that my own distrust of people protected us from her trailing me to the hotel that night. If she had…there's no telling what she would have done after seeing you and glee enter the hotel room with me. The woman is unscrupulous, and she doesn't care who she hurts in the process."

The possibility of glee getting caught up in all of this, after everything she's done for me, is infuriating. I can't let another soul suffer because of my mother.

I can't.

"What do you think she wants from you?" Samantha asks.

"Other than to torture me?" I laugh miserably. "I'm not sure. But she was strategic, attacking those closest to me, so it's obvious she wants to strip away my defenses before she takes her final blow."

Samantha shudders. "It's hard to believe you're related to her. The two of you are complete opposites."

I say nothing, because she's wrong. I'm quite capable of following in my mother's footsteps. I read people well, but rather than tear them down, I'm interested in helping them grow.

It's part of the reason I'm so determined to train Samantha.

"Since my mother must be caught within a hundred yards of me for the police to enforce the restraining order, I'll need you to act as the bait to draw her in."

"Not a problem. I'll do anything to help."

I warn her, "This could be dangerous, Samantha. There's no telling what my mother might do."

"Are you afraid she'll become violent?"

"I plan to provoke her, so I'm prepared for it. And that's why you must promise not to step in, no matter what happens."

Samantha huffs. "Thane, I'm more than capable of

defending myself."

"I agree but, for this plan to work, you can't get involved. You're only there to reel her in."

I don't say it out loud, but I am willing to die to protect Samantha if things go south.

Several days later, the Beast finally contacts her, and Samantha dutifully plays the tearful, helpless woman to get her to agree to meet off campus. With the place and time set, Anderson and Durov join me to scope out the area and finalize our plans.

I've purposely kept Samantha in the dark so she won't be implicated should my mission fail. The less she knows, the better—she's taking a big enough risk for me.

"Durov, Samantha's safety is our first priority. No matter how this goes down, I want you to stay focused on protecting her."

The Russian slams his fist into his palm. "Do not worry, comrade. My charge will be protected."

"Anderson, as you know, the timing of the call is vital, and you must sound convincing. If the cops suspect she's been set up, I could be the one going to jail today."

"Not going to happen, buddy. I've got this."

I'm confident in both men, and I trust Samantha to keep her promise not to intervene. The only unknown is the Beast herself, and I know from personal experience how treacherous she can be.

Despite my best efforts to hold the memory back, an

overwhelming feeling of dread paralyzes me as I recall running up the stairs to my parent's bedroom…

I burst into their bedroom and instantly stop in my tracks when I see my father pointing a gun directly at my mother.

She's lying in their bed—in the arms of another man.

My father vacillates between pointing the gun at her and at the boy toy who seems frozen with fear.

With a voice full of pain, my father asks, "Why?"

My mother glares at him as if the circumstances have been reversed and *she* is the one who has been betrayed. Rather than answer, my mother says nothing. She acts as if the question doesn't even rate a response.

"*Papà…*" I choke out, fighting the painful lump growing in my throat.

When he looks in my direction, the raw devastation I see in his eyes chills me to the bone. If only I had warned him about her, this wouldn't be happening right now.

My father's hand trembles as he keeps the gun pointed at his wife, looking as if he's about to shoot her. But then, after several tense moments, he lowers the gun and confesses to her, "I could never shoot you."

"Why? Because you love me, Alonzo?" she scoffs. "I don't love you."

He stares at her in silence with tears in his eyes.

My mother remains unaffected and growls in irritation. "Enough with the dramatics." Her face slowly transforms into something truly terrifying as her lips curl into a cruel smile. She challenges him in an icy voice ripe with disdain, "Go ahead. Pull the trigger and end this charade for both of us."

I can't breathe when my father turns toward me. "I'm sorry, son."

Before I can move, he puts the gun to his head and pulls the trigger.

I scream in horror as I watch his body fall limply to the floor. Running to him, I cradle his head in my lap, ignoring the gushing blood and fragments of bone as I beg him to hold on.

"Call the fucking ambulance!" I yell at my mother.

When I look back and see his eyes blink, I feel a moment of hope. "*Papà*, you've got to hang on until the ambulance gets here. You're going to be okay."

But, all that blood scares me…

His gaze starts drifting slowly around the room until it finally locks on me. "Thane…" He blinks several more times, his breaths becoming slower and fainter.

He's leaving me, and there is nothing I can do about it.

"Don't die, *Papà*. I need you."

My father's gaze remains on me. "*Ti amo,*" he whispers.

I can't hold back the sob when I answer, "I love you, too."

"I'm sorry, son…" He continues to stare up at me as his life slowly ebbs away. His body suddenly stiffens, and I hear the horrifying sound of the death rattle as my father takes his final breath.

At the young age of fifteen, I watch helplessly as the light disappears from my father's eyes.

Before the appointed time, the three of us take our positions and wait for Samantha to arrive. She comes early, sitting down at the designated bench.

To keep up the ruse of her fragile state, Samantha keeps looking around nervously and dabbing her eyes as if she's crying.

My mother, ever the control freak, arrives fifteen minutes late. I suspect she's been scoping out the area to make sure there aren't any surprises waiting for her, but she has no idea who she is dealing with.

I'm no longer the hurt little boy she abandoned years ago. No, I am every bit as dangerous as she is.

When the Beast finally shows herself, I'm struck by the fact that she is just as beautiful as I remember. I hate that she appears to be thriving, despite causing her husband's suicide and abandoning her only son soon after it.

I let my growing anger add fuel to the fire.

The Beast approaches the bench wearing a smug look on her face, confident in her power over Samantha. I can't hear what they're saying but wait patiently until she gives me the signal.

While Samantha keeps the Beast occupied with her tearful confessions, I walk up unnoticed, my heart beating rapidly as I approach.

I never thought I would see this woman again—and now I am about to look the Beast in the eye. Although it pains me to say the word aloud, I call out, "Mother."

I see her back stiffen before she slowly turns to face me. She forces a smile, but it's not lost on me that her eyes remain cold and distant even though the tone of her voice is warm. "Thane, I've missed you."

Her eyes dart around, however, realizing she's been set up. I enjoy seeing her squirm for once.

She looks back at Samantha and says accusingly, "Did you know he was coming?"

Samantha stares at me as if she's truly terrified. "No!" She looks at my mother in desperation. "How did he find us? Please, Ruth, you have to protect me from your son."

Samantha's acting is convincing, leaving my mother unsure and confused. She turns back to me, faking a calm demeanor. "I'm surprised to see you here. Especially, after you've avoided me the last few years."

I say nothing, but smile at her with the same cruel smile she gave my father when she told him to pull the trigger.

*A son never forgets.*

Keeping up the ruse as Samantha's defender, my mother demands, "Why have you been harassing this girl? It's disgusting and indefensible."

"I like hurting people, Mother. It's the only joy I have in the world."

She looks me up and down, and I note with satisfaction the fear in her eyes. "Don't play games with me."

"I don't play games," I answer, my eyes reflecting the violence I've longed to inflict on her. "You didn't realize your little boy was all grown up now. And I've had years to fantasize about what I would do when I saw you again."

I notice Samantha shifting uncomfortably on the bench. She had no idea she would be coming face to face with this side of me.

"Thane, stop this," the Beast demands. Turning to Samantha for sympathy, she cries, "I told you he was dangerous."

Samantha says nothing.

As I take a step toward my mother, I'm gratified to see her instinctually take a step back from me.

I am in control here.

For the first time in her life, the Beast knows real fear.

"I'm glad you've made this easy for me, Mother."

"What do you mean?" she barks, trying to cover her fear with anger.

"Who would blame you? A mother who lost her husband to suicide because she was caught in bed fucking another man might suddenly feel the weight of his death on her soul."

"Liar!" She turns to Samantha. "He's a goddamn liar!"

"Maybe that same woman can't stand the sight of herself knowing that she abandoned her only son after her husband's death, because she would rather fuck other men than be a mother."

"Don't twist what happened. You father was the

whore, not me."

"So, after living with that guilt for years, she finally realizes there's only one way to make it right."

I move in closer as I say, "Taking the knife, she vows to make things right and cuts her veins so all that bad blood can run out."

My mother snarls. "I am *not* a coward like your father. I would never kill myself."

"Maybe it isn't the mother who makes things right…maybe it's the son who helps her do the right thing."

Her face goes completely white.

"I have a knife waiting for you."

She stares at me, trying desperately to read my face for any indication that I'm bluffing. But I'm fully committed to my role, remembering what it was like when I saw the light die in my father's eyes.

I can see her survival instincts kicking in—it's either kill or be killed.

She pulls out a gun from her purse.

The blood starts pumping through my veins. My only goal now is to keep her focused on me to protect Samantha.

Pointing the gun at my chest, she says, "As you can clearly see, Samantha, my life is being threatened. I have no other choice but to protect myself."

Samantha remains silent, her eyes fixed on the gun.

I smile again, looking deep into my mother's eyes. "Do you see how much I hate you, Mother?"

Her hand starts trembling, so she grasps the gun with both hands trying to keep it steady.

I slowly raise my hands up in surrender. What makes me dangerous is that I don't care if she shoots, and she can sense that.

"Go ahead, Mother."

"All I wanted was to have my son back. But you...you've turned into a monster."

"Yes, Mother. I've turned into you."

Curling her upper lip in disgust, she takes aim. "No. You're as weak as your fath—"

"This is the police. Put the gun down now!" The sound of guns being cocked fills the air around us.

Unlike me, the Beast is afraid to die, and I watch with gratification as she drops the gun and it clatters onto the cement.

The police move in quickly, patting her down before forcing her hands behind her back to handcuff her.

I slowly lower my hands, not quite believing it's worked.

After patting me down and finding no weapons, the police officer asks if I'm okay. I nod in answer, but then look at Samantha and ask him to check on my friend.

As I watch the Beast being led away in handcuffs, I feel a profound sense of justice.

Once everyone is gone and we're alone again, Samantha holds her hand out to me. "You were brilliant, Thane. That speech you gave your mother gave me goosebumps."

I deflect her compliment, not wanting to acknowledge that side of myself. "You were convincing, Samantha—and exceedingly brave."

"When the police arrived and she was pointing the gun at you with your hands up, that was the perfect setup. But I have to admit I was terrified for you."

To ease her mind, I lie. "She only carries the gun for show."

"Well, it was an honor to help take the bitch down."

Shaking her hand firmly, I tell her with deep gratitude, "I couldn't have done it without you."

I remain behind after she leaves, wanting to talk to Anderson and Durov, who've remained in hiding. Durov walks out first, clapping his hands loudly. "That was a beautiful thing to watch."

Anderson follows behind, adding, "I'm fucking impressed, Davis. It played out exactly the way you said it would."

I grin with satisfaction, exhilarated by our success as I shake both their hands. "With you guys behind me, the Beast never stood a chance."

Durov, ever the Casanova, raises an eyebrow. "*Moy droog*, why did you not tell me your friend is incredibly beautiful?"

"Oh, so *now* you want to meet Samantha?" I ask, chuckling.

He shakes his head. "If she's still training as a Dominant, there would be no point. I refuse to be topped."

"You never know...you might like it," Anderson jokes.

Durov throws his head back, laughing. "*Nyet*. This Russian submits to no one."

# Brush with Fate

N ow that the Beast is gone, I can finally focus on the semester finals looming ahead. Unfortunately, my concentration has suffered since she re-entered my life, so I must double up my efforts.

"Buddy, you're worrying me again."

"How so?" I ask, looking up from my textbook.

"You haven't left this room all week. It's like we're back to the beginning of the school year."

"You can thank my mother for that," I grumble as I return my attention to my Economics textbook.

"How about we spend tonight at the dungeon? Give that big brain of yours a rest?"

"No. I still have a paper to finish, and I'll need to pull an all-nighter to do that."

Staring at the half-eaten apple on my desk, he shakes his head. "I bet you haven't been eating, either."

"Food is a time-waster, but I promise to stuff my face once finals are over." I look up from my textbook. "What I really need right now is peace and quiet so I can prepare for the exam today."

He *tsks* at me. "By those dark circles under your eyes, I'd say you need a week's worth of rest and relaxation."

I growl in frustration. "What do I have to do to get you to shut up? I just told you I need to study."

He points at me and smiles. "You're cranky because you need to eat."

I snarl. "I'm cranky because you won't shut the fuck up."

Anderson chuckles. "I know you've looked over that textbook three times already. There isn't any new information that's going to magically appear."

"I can't afford not to do well on the exam. My grade is hinging on a top score."

"I know what will guarantee the excellent score you seek."

I'm not amused and glare at him, realizing he isn't going to leave me alone.

"If you go into that test without eating, all your hard work and study have been for nothing." He walks over and closes my textbook. "So come with me and let's get something for lunch."

"I don't have time." With all this talk of food, my stomach betrays me by growling.

He raises an eyebrow, stating smugly, "See?"

"Will you shut up the rest of the week if I have lunch with you now?"

"Sure."

"Fine!" I huff angrily, standing up. Naturally, my stomach starts aching with hunger pains as if to prove Anderson right. "Let's get this over with."

I assume we're headed to the cafeteria where I can grab a sandwich and another apple before heading back to the dorm, but Anderson walks to the bus stop, instead.

"I don't have time for this."

He puts his hand on my shoulder. "You need to nourish that body with wholesome food like my mama cooks. This place isn't far, and you're going to thank me later. Trust me."

I want to bail, but the damn bus pulls up, so I reluctantly get on and sit down. Luckily, it's a straight shot, and fifteen minutes later Anderson gets of the bus, pointing at a diner.

I'm immediately assaulted by delicious smells as I follow him into the restaurant, and it makes the ache in my stomach triple in intensity. I slide into the nearest booth to grab a menu.

"You can't go wrong with a chicken fried steak," Anderson tells me. "But I personally recommend the chicken and waffles."

I look at him skeptically. "That's an odd combination."

"I *know*. Thought the same thing myself. But it's a popular southern dish and, damn, it's good."

I suspect Anderson isn't suggesting, but telling me, what I will be ordering for lunch. However, at this point, I don't care because the hunger pains are getting decidedly worse.

Thankfully, the waitress is quick to take our order.

While we wait, I look around the diner and notice a number of older folk reading newspapers, along with several families enjoying their lunch together. One of the kids stands out because a girl with pigtails and a polka-dot dress is laughing for no apparent reason. When the father catches me looking in their direction, he glares harshly at me.

I turn back to Anderson and ask, "When's the food getting here?"

"Hold your horses. We just ordered. Here, have a packet of sugar to tide you over," he says, throwing one at me.

"Very funny."

I look down at the packet, however, half-tempted to open it and pour the sugar into my mouth. I have to resist the urge until my plate of food arrives.

The savory smell of the fried chicken has my mouth watering. But then Anderson has the nerve to pour maple syrup over it.

"What the hell?"

The father who was glaring at me barks from his booth, "Language!"

I hold my hand up to let him know it won't happen again, then growl at Anderson, "Why did you ruin my chicken by covering it in syrup?"

"Just take a bite."

With my stomach growling, I bite into the flesh, appreciating the satisfying crunch of the skin. Oddly, the sweetness of the maple syrup complements the savory aspect of the chicken. Although I like it, I give him a look of disgust. "Thanks for ruining my meal."

Anderson grins as he watches me devour the entire meal in a matter of minutes. "Yeah, I can see how much

I ruined it for you."

I sit back in my seat, my stomach now full and satisfied.

As I watch Anderson finish consuming his meal, I feel a tug of remorse. "Look, I know I give you no end of crap, but I appreciate how you look out for me."

Anderson reaches over and ruffles my hair. "You're like the nerdy kid brother I never had."

I chuckle. "Even though the semester's not over, I think it's fair to say you've won our bet."

He looks at me, stunned. "Seriously?"

"Yeah. I concede there's a life beyond college and getting my degree."

He gives me a half-grin. "You want to know something funny?"

"Sure."

"The last few weeks when I said I was out 'partying,' I was actually in the library studying. I just didn't want you to know."

"It's not possible," I say laughing. "I *know* you're playing me right now."

"I'm completely serious, man. Turns out that when I apply myself, I'm actually good with numbers." He shrugs. "In fact, I've already looked into taking that Applied Calculus class next semester."

"I never would have guessed," I tell him, but inwardly I smile, silently congratulating myself that my subtle nudges throughout the year have finally led him to this realization.

Rather than tell him that was my plan all along, I let him have the win.

Anderson glances at his watch and his eyes dart to the bus stop. "We gotta go. The bus will be here any minute."

"Let me get your check."

"Nah, you don't have to cover for me. I brought cash."

"I want to."

Anderson slaps me on the back. "Thanks, buddy!" As he starts toward the door, he warns me, "You better hurry, though. We can't miss this bus, or we'll miss the start of exams."

"I'll be there in a minute," I assure him. "And, if I don't make it, tell the bus driver to wait."

"I'll be damned if I'm holding the bus for your slow ass, even if you *are* buying lunch," he answers with a grin, pushing the door open as he heads out.

I go to the counter and give the waitress the cash for our two checks. While I wait for the change, I notice the little girl with the pigtails standing beside me. She's small, not more than seven, and is having a heck of a time trying to grab a container of catsup from the counter. Her tongue is sticking out from the effort as she stands on tiptoes with her arm fully extended, trying to grab the bottle. Despite her determination, it remains just out of the reach of her grasping fingers.

I slide the bottle over to her and give her a friendly wink.

She grabs it, clutching the bottle to her chest as she grins up at me. "Thank you, Mister!"

The kid's smile is infectious, and I chuckle kindly. "No problem, kid."

"Guess where I'm going."

I shake my head, charmed by the little brunette's enthusiasm.

Her hazel eyes sparkle with childish delight when she tells me, "I'm going to Disneyland for the first time. Have you ever been?"

"Can't say I have."

"You should, you know! They have Mickey and Minnie…and Pluto. I love, love, love Pluto," she tells me in a singsong voice.

"Well, with Pluto there, I'm sure you're bound to have a good time."

I hear her father's stern voice from the table as he barks, "Get back here, young lady." I glance over to see her overprotective father glaring at me again.

"Yes, Daddy," the tiny brunette answers, skipping over to the table with the catsup bottle still clutched to her chest.

As I watch the young girl slide into the booth, I overhear her mother say, "How many times have we told you not to talk to strangers?"

I can feel the heat of the father's distrustful stare burning a hole in my back as I turn to face the waitress while she counts back my change. I lay the four bucks on the counter as a tip, thrusting the coins into my jeans pocket.

As I pass by the family on my way out, the little girl chirps, "Thanks for the 'sup, Mister."

I smile. "Anytime, kid."

"Not another word, Brianna Renee Bennett," the father barks angrily.

I chuckle to myself, shaking my head as I push the door open and head out.

*You really need to chill, man. It's not like I'm going to molest your little girl...*

# One Door Closes

As I watch everyone packing up to move out for the summer, I feel an ache of genuine sadness. Although I thrive on the challenge of classes and will miss that over the summer months, it's the interactions with my friends I will miss more.

It's hard to believe it's only been a year, when I look at the changes in me. At the start of the year, I never imagined I would find myself in this position—not wanting to leave this small, cramped dorm room.

I look at my desk which I had strategically placed next to the tiny window. I thought that desk would become my whole world. I had no idea then what was in store for me.

I run my fingers over the words *I love Sherry* carved into the wood.

I'm going to miss this old desk...

"What are you looking all misty-eyed for?" Anderson asks, pulling out his storage trunk from under the bed.

I shrug. "Just feeling nostalgic."

"I've got some nostalgia for ya." He opens his trunk and takes out the partially empty bottle of whiskey he's kept hidden all this time and sets it down on his desk.

"Remember this?"

I smile. "I certainly do."

"Well, I think we should finish it. What do you say?"

"By all means."

Anderson gets out two glasses and pours a generous amount into each, finishing off the last of his grandfather's whiskey.

"To good friends," he says, holding up his glass.

"The best," I reply, clinking my glass against his.

We both take a sip and sigh in pleasure at the same time. Anderson points at me. "We've become like an old couple."

"Maybe it's good we're taking a break, before we start finishing each other's sentences."

He slaps his thigh. "That's exactly what I was thinking. Scary…"

I laugh as I take a long draught of the smooth whiskey. "Someday, I'll repay you for sharing your grandfather's whiskey with me."

"No need to. I told Granddad about you, and he said that's how he wanted it to be used. He's sending me back here with another bottle next year."

"Can I be your roommate?" I joke.

"That was never a question, buddy. I'll need your help with that Advanced Calc class.

"Oh, so I'm just being used for my math abilities."

"Why else would I put up with you?"

I laugh. "Why, indeed?"

"So, what are your plans over the summer?"

"My uncle wants to do some renovations with their house, so I volunteered to assist him since he's fronting the money for my education. What about you?"

"Like you, I'm going to be helping my dad with chores around the ranch."

"And tickling cows?"

He winks at me. "I'm sure old Betsy wouldn't mind, but I have my sights set on a few girls I knew in high school. I'm thinking this summer might prove interesting."

"I'm jealous."

"Right...Not buying it when you can visit the dungeon every night of the week."

I nod. "I'm thinking of staying with Durov over the weekends. He told me his family plans on buying that beach house he's renting."

"Shit...to have that kind of money would be amazing."

"Agreed, but he tells me it doesn't make the kind of difference you would think. With money comes a lot of pressure."

"I'd like to know what that pressure feels like," he chuckles, taking another sip of the whiskey.

"And there's no reason you can't. With a head for business, you could go far."

"I'll drink to that!" he says, clinking his glass against mine before downing the last of his whiskey. "Maybe we'll even work together, you and me."

"Who knows? Stranger things have happened."

There's a light knock on the door.

I quickly finish the last of my drink while Anderson shoves the bottle and glasses into his trunk before shutting it. He walks over to door and calls out in a humorous voice, "Who is it?"

The person on the other side hesitates for a moment before answering. "The Reynolds. We're Davis's uncle and aunt."

Anderson immediately throws the door open as I stand up.

"Welcome, and please come in," he tells them, taking my uncle's hand and shaking it. "You have helped raise a fine boy here."

To my aunt, he says, "And, you, Mrs. Reynolds. You make the best darn brownies I've ever had."

She blushes. "Why thank you, young man."

I walk over and hug them both before formally introducing them to Anderson.

"It's such a pleasure to finally meet you, Mr. Anderson," my aunt gushes.

"The pleasure is all mine, ma'am," Anderson says, giving her a wink.

My aunt's giggles fill the room.

"So, Davis, are you ready to go or do you need some more time?" my uncle asks.

"You can call me Thane, Unc." I nod my head toward Anderson. "He's cool."

"Oh, that's a relief," my aunt exclaims. "It's so hard to remember to call you Davis. I'm bound to mess it up if I try."

I give her another hug. "Thankfully, it's not an issue anymore, Auntie."

"Why's that?" my uncle asks, sounding interested.

Neither of them knows about my mother's presence on campus, and I would like to keep it that way. They've been through enough because of me.

"Nobody cares who this big knucklehead is," Anderson answers for me, rubbing the top of my head. And, with that, the question is dropped without the need for further explanation.

My aunt's eyes twinkle with delight. "I just love seeing you happy, honey."

I nod to her, realizing how much I owe her for sticking by me through those dark days. I didn't make it easy on her—on either of them.

"I'm pretty much packed, Unc. I didn't bring much to begin with."

He chuckles. "I know. I remember you took it up yourself with no help from us."

"Well, I don't mind a little help these days," I tell him, handing him the garment bag with all my suits.

"Do you have anything for me?" my aunt asks hopefully.

I look around my spare room and shrug, having only the large suitcase.

"I might have something, Auntie Reynolds," Anderson tells her.

I can't believe it when he grabs his cowboy hat from his closet and puts it on his head before pulling out his miniature bullwhip. "Thane, buddy, you don't mind keeping Myrtle while I'm gone, do ya?"

My aunt's eyes grow wide when he hands her the bullwhip.

"Wow. I've never seen one of these in real life before, much less touched one."

"I'd be mighty obliged if you would help Thane keep her safe for me."

"It'll be my pleasure."

"Thank you, kindly," he says, giving her another wink.

I cannot believe how thick Anderson can lay on the cowboy charm. He has my aunt eating out of his hand.

"Hey, Unc. Anderson and I planned a quick meet up with friends. After we get this stuff in the car, do you mind if I cut out for a few?"

"Not at all, Thane. Take as much time as you need."

I look around the room wistfully. "I'm going to miss this place."

"But, remember," my aunt says, smiling at me, "when one door closes, another one opens."

"True enough, Auntie."

Durov is already there waiting for us in the commons area.

"So, this is the big farewell for the cattleman. Off to play with the cows in Colorado, are you?" he laughs, flicking Anderson's hat.

"Watch it," Anderson growls good-naturedly.

"A farewell and an introduction," I tell Durov. "I want you to meet Samantha before she heads out, since you were the one who suggested I start training her."

"How is that going, comrade?"

"It's going well, but we've only had the one session so far because of the whole Beast incident. However, I've planned out several more to do over the summer since she lives in the area."

"I'm glad to hear that it's working out for you."

I think I see Samantha in the distance and wave.

When she starts in our direction, I tell Durov, "Be on your best behavior. She told me she's nervous about meeting you."

As she draws near, I'm surprised to see she's wearing a tight, red, A-line skirt and tall stilettos. Confidence oozes from Samantha as she walks over to us, her stilettos echoing seductively with each step.

Anderson growls under his breath, "Well, hello, beautiful…"

Durov says nothing as she approaches, but I can see he's captivated by her.

After I make the introductions, I'm totally unprepared when the Russian suddenly takes her hand and brings it to his lips.

"So, we finally meet…"

I look over at Anderson, who looks as shocked as I feel. Hell, he and I might as well not be there, the two are *that* intense as they gaze into each other's eyes.

Cracking a joke at Durov's expense, Anderson asks, "So, tell me. Why *do* you shave your head? Is it a Russian thing, or is it because you're losing your hair?"

Durov glances at me briefly before answering. "Actually, I lost someone recently and shaved it off in mourning."

Anderson looks embarrassed and quickly mutters, "Sorry for your loss, man. I didn't know…"

"I'm sorry, too," Samantha says, finally breaking her silence. "However, I think you look incredibly sexy without hair."

Durov rubs his hand over his smooth head and smirks at her. "So, you like bald Russians, do you?"

I see a blush rise on Samantha's cheeks. "Perhaps," she answers as a seductive smile plays across her blood-red lips.

The chemistry between the two is so intense, it's as if I can see sparks flying off them as they continue to stare at each other.

However, I know Samantha hates cocky alphas and Durov has zero interest in partnering with a Dominant. Still, the level of their chemistry is off the charts.

There is no possible way it can work between them.

And all I can think is:

*Let the fireworks begin…*

I hope you enjoyed *Sir's Rise!*

Coming next—***Master's Fate: Rise of the Dominants Book Two***, the 2nd of the trilogy

The story of these young Doms has just begun!

Find out what happens to Master Anderson, Sir, Rytsar and Samantha as they start their second year of college.

FIREWORKS!

Read the next book!

Or, if you are new to Brie and the gang, you can begin the journey with the 1st Box Set of ***Brie's Submission*** which is FREE!

Read the 1st box set

# COMING NEXT

## *Master's Fate:*
## Rise of the Dominants Book Two

Reviews mean the world to me!

I truly appreciate you taking the time to review
**Sir's Rise**.

If you could leave a review on both Goodreads and the site where you purchased this eBook from, I would be so grateful. Sincerely, ~Red

Don't miss the stories of the Sir, Rytsar, Master Anderson, and Samantha that you read about in
**Sir's Rise.**

Don't miss the other book in the trilogy!

### The Russian Reborn, Final Book

You can begin the next part of the journey for Sir, Rytsar and Master Anderson with the 1$^{st}$ Box Set of *Brie's Submission* which is FREE!

Start reading NOW!

# ABOUT THE AUTHOR

Over Two Million readers have enjoyed Red's stories

**Red Phoenix – USA Today Bestselling Author**
**Winner of 8 Readers' Choice Awards**

## Hey Everyone!

I'm Red Phoenix, an author who also happens to be a submissive in real life. I wrote the Brie's Submission series because I wanted people everywhere to know just how much fun BDSM can be.

There is a huge cast of characters who are part of Brie's journey. The further you read into the story the more you learn about each one. I hope you grow to love Brie and the gang as much as I do.

They've become like family.

When I'm not writing, you can find me online with readers.

I heart my fans! ~Red

**To find out more visit my Website**

redphoenixauthor.com

**Follow Me on BookBub**

bookbub.com/authors/red-phoenix

**Newsletter: Sign up**

redphoenixauthor.com/newsletter-signup

**Facebook: AuthorRedPhoenix**

**Twitter: @redphoenix69**

**Instagram: RedPhoenixAuthor**

**I invite you to join my reader Group**!

facebook.com/groups/539875076052037

SIGN UP FOR MY NEWSLETTER
HERE FOR THE LATEST RED
PHOENIX UPDATES

SALES, GIVEAWAYS, NEW
RELEASES, EXCLUSIVE SNEAK
PEEKS, AND MORE!
SIGN UP HERE
REDPHOENIXAUTHOR.COM/NEWSLETTER-
SIGNUP

# Red Phoenix is the author of:

## Brie's Submission Series:
Teach Me #1
Love Me #2
Catch Me #3
Try Me #4
Protect Me #5
Hold Me #6
Surprise Me #7
Trust Me #8
Claim Me #9
Enchant Me #10
A Cowboy's Heart #11
Breathe with Me #12
Her Russian Knight #13
Under His Protection #14
Her Russian Returns #15
In Sir's Arms #16
Bound by Love #17
Tied to Hope #18

**\*You can also purchase the** AUDIO BOOK **Versions**

Also part of the Submissive Training Center world:

Captain's Duet
Safe Haven #1
Destined to Dominate #2

Rise of the Dominates Trilogy
Sir's Rise #1
Master's Fate #2
The Russian Reborn #3

# Other Books by Red Phoenix

---

*Blissfully Undone*
\* Available in eBook and paperback

(Snowy Fun—Two people find themselves snowbound in a cabin where hidden love can flourish, taking one couple on a sensual journey into ménage à trois)

---

*His Scottish Pet: Dom of the Ages*
\* Available in eBook and paperback

Audio Book: *His Scottish Pet: Dom of the Ages*

(Scottish Dom—A sexy Dom escapes to Scotland in the late 1400s. He encounters a waif who has the potential to free him from his tragic curse)

---

*The Erotic Love Story of Amy and Troy*
\* Available in eBook and paperback

(Sexual Adventures—True love reigns, but fate continually throws Troy and Amy into the arms of others)

# eBooks

*Varick: The Reckoning*

(Savory Vampire—A dark, sexy vampire story. The hero navigates the dangerous world he has been thrust into with lusty passion and a pure heart)

———————————

*Keeper of the Wolf Clan (Keeper of Wolves, #1)*

(Sexual Secrets—A virginal werewolf must act as the clan's mysterious Keeper)

———————————

*The Keeper Finds Her Mate (Keeper of Wolves, #2)*

(Second Chances—A young she-wolf must choose between old ties or new beginnings)

———————————

*The Keeper Unites the Alphas (Keeper of Wolves, #3)*

(Serious Consequences—The young she-wolf is captured by the rival clan)

———————————

*Boxed Set: Keeper of Wolves Series (Books 1-3)*

(Surprising Secrets—A secret so shocking it will rock Layla's world. The young she-wolf is put in a position of being able to save her werewolf clan or becoming the reason for its destruction)

———————————

*Socrates Inspires Cherry to Blossom*

(Satisfying Surrender—A mature and curvaceous woman becomes fascinated by an online Dom who has much to teach her)

---

*By the Light of the Scottish Moon*

(Saving Love—Two lost souls, the Moon, a werewolf, and a death wish…)

---

*In 9 Days*

(Sweet Romance—A young girl falls in love with the new student, nicknamed "the Freak")

---

*9 Days and Counting*

(Sacrificial Love—The sequel to *In 9 Days* delves into the emotional reunion of two longtime lovers)

---

*And Then He Saved Me*

(Saving Tenderness—When a young girl tries to kill herself, a man of great character intervenes with a love that heals)

---

*Play With Me at Noon*

(Seeking Fulfillment—A desperate wife lives out her fantasies by taking five different men in five days)

# Connect with Red on Substance B

**Substance B** is a platform for independent authors to directly connect with their readers. Please visit Red's Substance B page where you can:

- Sign up for Red's newsletter
- Send a message to Red
- See all platforms where Red's books are sold

Visit Substance B today to learn more about your favorite independent authors.

www.ingramcontent.com/pod-product-compliance
Lightning Source LLC
Chambersburg PA
CBHW071756190726
48292CB00003B/996